SHELF LIFE

DOUGLAS CLARK

Also available in Perennial Library
by Douglas Clark:

POACHER'S BAG
ROAST EGGS
SICK TO DEATH

SHELF LIFE

DOUGLAS CLARK

PERENNIAL LIBRARY

Harper & Row, Publishers

New York, Cambridge, Philadelphia, San Francisco
London, Mexico City, São Paulo, Sydney

A hardcover edition of this book is published by Victor Gollancz
Ltd. in London, England. It is here reprinted by arrangement
with John Farquharson, Ltd.

First PERENNIAL LIBRARY edition published 1983.

LIBRARY OF CONGRESS CATALOG CARD NUMBER: 83-47581

ISBN: 0-06-080675-3

83 84 85 86 87 10 9 8 7 6 5 4 3 2 1

For Meriel

SHELF LIFE

DOUGLAS CLARK

Chapter 1

Sergeant Tom Watson, standing behind the desk in Colesworth police station, looked up with a growl of wrath. "Watch it, Sutcliffe."

Constable Sutcliffe had slung his cheese-cutter uniform cap on to the counter so violently that it had skidded along the smooth surface, past the ledger Watson had been working on, and had then continued until fetched up by a telephone which had uttered a ping of protest against such treatment.

"Sorry, Sarge. It's just . . ." Sutcliffe didn't finish. He was obviously too put-out to describe his frustration in words.

"What's got your rag out?" asked Watson, recognising his subordinate's plight.

"Those bloody magistrates, Sarge. Lot of do-gooding old women, they are. No wonder there's so much crime with a load of old cagmags like that on the bench."

"You haven't put your foot in it again, have you? Not with Inspector Snell prosecuting?"

"No, Sarge."

"What, then?"

"Those three young villains, Boyce, Lawson and Mobb . . ."

"What about them?"

"They've only let them off."

"What did you expect, lad? It's their first crime."

"Detected, Sarge, maybe. But look!"

"I've no need to look, Sutcliffe. I know. They've broken into at least five houses in the last month. It became a local scandal because the coppers couldn't nick 'em. Then, when we do nab them, they're let off by a lot of old fuddies who pat them on the head

7

and tell them not to do it again. But that's life, lad. It's produced a society that favours villains and disheartens eager young coppers like you just when you feel you've done a good job of work. That's what you thought, isn't it, when you ran in that bunch of young tearaways that's just been let off?"

"It makes me sick, Sarge. I got 'em red-handed. I'd seen what they'd done to those other houses. Urinated on the carpets, smeared the walls, smashed furniture and fittings—just for the hell of it."

"I know, lad, but you stopped them from doing it in that last house, didn't you? So you couldn't tell all that to the court."

"Well . . ."

"Pity you didn't let 'em get on with it before you nabbed 'em. Then you'd have had something to tell the magistrates."

Sutcliffe waved his arms in protest. "We're supposed to prevent crime, Sarge."

"You'll learn, lad. You know, I know, and Inspector Snell knows those three pulled those other jobs. It was because we all knew that—but had no proof—that you were told off to keep an eye on them. So you caught them at the fifth time of asking. But you weren't allowed to tell the court all that. Stands to reason, doesn't it?"

"That's my point, Sarge. The inspector laid the law down. Wouldn't let me even hint at the other jobs."

"He daren't, lad. Those three had a smart-arse lawyer there to see you didn't. He'd have had you and Inspector Snell by the short and curlies if you'd as much as opened your mouth to breathe a word about the previous break-ins. It isn't justice, lad, but it's the law. And the sooner you learn the difference, the sooner you'll learn to let yobbos like that do a bit of damage before running them in. Then you'll have a case."

"They'd still have got away as first offenders."

"True. But they'd have got a suspended sentence and if they'd put a foot wrong after that they'd have been properly on the hook."

This did little to comfort Sutcliffe. "Pity they didn't vandalise one of those magistrates' homes," he muttered.

"The result would still have been the same, lad. Any magistrate

8

who'd been on the receiving end wouldn't be allowed to sit when the case came up. I don't have to tell you that."

"I know, Sarge. But surely all those J.P.s—if one of their mates had been done—would gun for three yobbos like Boyce, Lawson and Mobb."

"Grow up, Sutcliffe," growled Watson. "You've still got a lot to learn about life if you think that. Take Miss Foulger, for instance . . ."

"She was Chairman this morning."

"Aye! Well she'd laugh herself sick in private if old Mrs Hargreaves was vandalised—and vice versa. And some of the men are no better. There's as much jealousy and umptiness among that lot as anywhere else in Colesworth. One half of 'em would let off anybody who did down somebody in the other half."

"Is that really true, Sarge? I mean . . ."

"Take my word for it, lad. And take your cap as well. Get off home to that little missus of yours, not forgetting that I had to rearrange your duties because you had to go to court. You're on tonight. Only half-shift if you're lucky. If not . . ." The sergeant shrugged. "Trouble is, we don't know what to expect these days—or nights."

Sutcliffe put on his cap. Anger appeared to have given way to resignation. Watson seemed to sense it. He said: "Don't let it stop you keeping an eye open for any more tricks those three may get up to—or anybody like them."

"Fat lot of good that will do, Sarge."

"Be off, lad. Go straight home and forget it."

"Can't go straight home, more's the pity."

"And why not?"

"Got to do some shopping."

"What's up? Wife not well?"

"A bit off colour. She went to the doctor. He's given her a prescription, but I've got to go right over to Park Street to get it made up."

"Of course. I was forgetting. Old Stanmore in the High Street's packing it in, isn't he?"

"He's not all that old, Sarge. Leastways he's not retiring age yet,

9

but he told me he'd been losing money for some years now, so he's closing. He tried to sell the business, but nobody would take it on."

"I'm not surprised. I read only the other day that we're losing chemists' shops at a rate of over two hundred a year. The chains are taking over. When did old Stanmore actually jack it in?"

"Last Saturday. He'd sold most of his stock—drugs and what-not—to other chemists before then. I saw him yesterday. He's cleaning the place out this week, then he hopes to let it."

"Who to?"

"He says there's an estate agent interested but they don't want to pay a good rent. I told him to sell it to a Building Society. They've got more branches round here than investors."

Watson shook his head. Whether it was to disagree or merely to express dismay at the state the country was coming to was not clear, but Sutcliffe took it as a general sign of approval for his own wisdom. He, in turn, grimaced to show his appreciation of such approbation and moved away to leave the station by the back door.

After the case in which Constable Sutcliffe had been concerned that morning, the magistrates dealt with two motoring offences and then were faced with hearing the case against Joe Howlett, tramp, of no known address except the great outdoors with occasional sojourns in one or other of H.M. prisons.

Despite the wide choice open to him, Howlett seemed to have a preference for Colesworth jail. It was comparatively small as prisons go, and never used for housing hard cases except, possibly, for a few days on remand. It was a friendly lock-up and suited Joe admirably whenever he felt in need of hospitality.

The Colesworth police had gently hauled Howlett in front of the bench at regular intervals over the years—always at the prisoner's own request. There was a set pattern. The old tramp would make a minor nuisance of himself until the police were obliged to take him in. He seemed to have a mind quite fertile in devising new forms of more or less harmless misdemeanour. This time he had held up the traffic in the road, just where it joined the south side of the Colesworth market place, by the simple expedient of doing a shuffle-dance in the middle of the not over-wide carriageway. The dance itself was performed in aged gumboots and—despite the summer weather—an old, torn, drab grey overcoat. Attached to strings round Joe's waist had been various badly-tied parcels and a couple of fire-blackened cans. He believed in carrying with him all his worldly goods which included a walking-stick with which he did a lot of the work that drew the crowd that was eventually to block both pavements.

So the police took him to court, but for Howlett the appearance was a disaster.

Miss Foulger, the Chairman of the bench, eyed him severely. As soon as the preliminary formalities were over and Joe had followed his usual custom of pleading guilty, Miss Foulger addressed him. Her tone was hard and matched her personality. She was over-poweringly masculine both in dress and demeanour. Despite the heat she was wearing what she called a costume, a jacket and skirt which had, nevertheless, been tailor-made out of men's suiting. Her hair was thick, pepper-and-salt grey and distinctly reminiscent of the bobbing and shingling era. She wore rimless spectacles with a black safety cord dangling from the earpieces.

"Howlett," she said severely, her well-fleshed face set as rigidly as a papier-mâché horror mask, "you have appeared in this court on more than a dozen previous occasions. The police officers who have had to deal with you have never wanted to bring you here but it is their opinion—and ours—that you have deliberately set out to oblige them to do so. I see from your records that you have always pleaded guilty, which attitude suggests to us that your sole intention on every occasion has been to secure for yourself a minor prison sentence for reasons known only to yourself.

"We have been playing your game too long, Howlett," she continued grimly. "We have invariably provided you with that which you sought. Now it is going to stop. The cost of keeping a man in prison is enormous. The taxpayers have been footing the bill for your penal sabbaticals long enough.

"This time you are not going to be sent to prison. You are going to be released. Let it be a warning to you. The next time you oblige the police to arrest you, you will be sentenced to work.

"Yes, to work, Howlett. That will not suit you, will it? You will be given community work to do. Digging and weeding in parks and gardens under close supervision." She put her hands together on the desk before her—large hands, lumpy with arthritis—and entwined her misshapen fingers. "There are many worthy citizens in Colesworth who, because of age or infirmity, need help such as you could give and for which they have already paid in supporting you in your years of idleness and misdemeanour."

She glanced sideways, first to Mrs Hargreaves on her right and then to the male member of the bench on her left. The whispered consultation was short and the conclusion unanimous, as indicated by the nodding of heads and grimaces of obvious displeasure with the disreputable figure before them.

"Why should you wish to go to prison, Howlett?" asked Mrs Hargreaves querulously. "I can understand you wishing to go there in the winter months, but not in the summer."

Joe Howlett mumbled some reply which was so lost in his matted beard that it was indecipherable to the magistrates.

"What did he say?"

The Clerk of the Court, somewhat nearer Howlett, looked up. "The prisoner replied, Your Worship, that everybody else takes a holiday in summer, so why shouldn't he?"

Mrs Hargreaves sniffed audibly, but had no retort to this except to label it as impertinence.

"No summer holiday for you, Howlett," said Miss Foulger firmly. "You will leave the court now. And don't forget that if you ever come back it will result in a long stint of back-breaking work."

The Clerk of the Court rose to formalise the decision of the bench.

"You heard what the lady said, Joe." Inspector Snell was more kindly than Miss Foulger as he stopped to speak to the tramp in the corridor outside the courtroom.

Howlett looked at him and replied: "Miserable old bitch."

"Hold it, Joe. It's your own fault for saying what you did. Why didn't you tell them you never try to get picked up unless you're out of food and flat broke? Why not tell them you've never claimed the dole or social security?"

12

Howlett snarled through his beard: "They're not worth talking to, Mr Snell. You know that. Look at them this morning. Letting off them three as had been caught to rights with enough mischief—nasty mischief—behind 'em to send a dozen other men inside for life."

"What do you know about them, Joe?" asked Snell quietly.

"There's not much goes on round here I don't know about, Mr Snell, as you well know."

"You're an old peeping-Tom, Joe."

"I keep my eyes open. An' just for nothing, Mr Snell, I reckon you ought to tell your Sergeant Watson—the one who's always on the desk in the nick . . ."

"Tell him what, Joe?"

"To watch out for that girl of his. She's keeping bad company."

"Pamela Watson is?"

Howlett nodded. "If that's her name, yes. Down in Burner's Wood with bad company."

The wood Howlett was referring to was more like a young forest and had, at one time, been the centre of the local charcoal-making industry—hence its name. It was dense with every type of timber, but still dotted with clearings where the fires had been made. Snell knew that Howlett spent much of his time there where some sort of shelter was easy to erect with plenty of material to hand and—very important to Howlett—where isolation and privacy were virtually assured.

"What's the name of this bad company?" demanded Snell who, before his promotion, had been a close colleague of Tom Watson and knew how much the sergeant doted on his teenage daughter. It would hurt Watson to think that the girl was running wild with undesirable characters.

"Come on, Joe, who with?"

"Seeing it's you, Mr Snell, and I've no quarrel with the cops . . ."

"I'm waiting."

"The three you had in court this morning."

Snell stared for a moment. Then—

"You're sure, Joe?" he asked quietly.

"Sometimes there's another girl with them. I've heard them call her Rosie Somebody-or-other."

Snell nodded. He knew Rosie. Rosie Sewell, a fast bit of goods. He hadn't known till now that she was a friend of Pam Watson's. He'd ask the sergeant if the two girls were pals. It would be a check on Joe's story.

"What do they get up to?" asked the inspector.

"Down to, you mean," retorted Howlett. "Actually I'm too shy to tell you." Snell had the impression that the tramp leered behind his beard. "But I *will* tell you this. The plastic groundsheet they hid away in a tree, where they thought it would be safe, came in mighty handy for the roof of my shelter."

"You've always sworn you don't nick things, Joe."

"Neither do I. But findings keepings. I don't nick and I don't drink. You know that, Mr Snell."

"I know it, Joe, otherwise I wouldn't give you this." The inspector drew a pound note from his hip pocket.

"There's no need, Mr Snell. I'll get by."

"You haven't got anything to eat, have you?"

"I'll get some scraps at the chip shop."

"Take this. I'll get it back at the nick—from the fund."

Howlett accepted the note and shuffled off. Snell turned to re-enter the courtroom but was buttonholed by the reporter from the local rag.

"Your constable was a bit put out this morning when those three youths got off scot-free."

"Wouldn't you have been a bit cross, Mr Bennett, if you'd got a scoop and somebody in authority—your editor—had killed it?"

"I get the analogy, Inspector. In those circumstances I reckon I would use language as strong as your young man did especially if, as I've heard, those three are the people who've been breaking into houses and vandalising them."

"Mr Bennett," said Snell, "you didn't hear that from my constable, and you won't hear it from me."

"No, of course not. But a nod is as good as a wink to a blind horse. If what I heard were to be true, for instance, the *Gazette* would stop asking why the police are doing nothing about these crimes—after we were given the nod that the locals had caught the villains but the bench had let them off, that is."

"Nothing doing, Mr Bennett. Sorry."

"Have it your way, Inspector."

"Sorry," said Snell again and turned away to re-enter the courtroom where he had more cases coming up.

Howlett's first place of call after leaving Snell had to be the police station where the bits and pieces of his so-called possessions would be awaiting collection.

"I heard you were out," said Sergeant Watson. "What kept you? Saying thank you to their worships, were you?"

Howlett asked: "Can I have my belongings?"

"That's what you call them, is it? Belongings? They're ready for you." He turned the book round on the desk. "You'll have to sign for them to say you got them back safely. Two tin cans, rusty, one with wire loop. Two tobacco tins, one containing eight non-safety matches, fourteen safety matches and the striking side of one safety matchbox. The other containing cigarette papers, dog ends, and a pinch of tobacco. Other items—one hank of twisted paper string, a broken penknife . . ."

Howlett accepted the proffered ball-point and signed his name—Joseph Porton Howlett.

"Ritzy sort of name, that," said Watson. Joe made no reply. Watson began to put the possessions on the desk. "I've put a dozen tea bags and a poke of sugar in your can."

"Thank you, Mr Watson. There was no need."

"We always know when you've got nothing, Joe."

"That woman . . ."

"What woman? Don't tell me you're courting, Joe?"

"The Foulger woman."

"Oh, her! You're the second who's had something to say about her this morning. And by the way, you didn't tell me what kept you after the case was over. Constable Brown, who nicked you, was back here a full quarter of an hour before you."

Joe Howlett picked up his cans. "Ask no questions, Mr Watson, and you'll get no lies told you. But I will tell you this, that woman

15

wants putting down. Straight she does."

Watson grew severe. "Don't you start to play any games, Joe. Not with her, especially. Otherwise you *will* find yourself in the nick—for good and all."

Howlett grunted, turned away and trudged out of the police station. The W.P.C. clerk, sitting at the typewriter on a small table behind Watson's desk counter, said: "What a nasty, smelly old man, Sergeant."

"What, him?" replied Watson. "Not half as smelly and nasty as some of the tricks pulled by most of the better-washed people we get in here. He doesn't break into houses to use sitting room carpets as lavatories, he doesn't get drunk, he doesn't bash people up and he doesn't go in for fraud, fiddling, illegal parking, speeding, driving without due care and attention or shoplifting."

The girl smiled. "You make him sound like a model citizen."

"Why not? He's an active conservationist."

"Him?"

"Yes. He makes good use of anything and everything."

Howlett, of course, had heard none of this. He had told Snell he would probably be able to get some scraps from the fish and chip shop. This was true enough. Jack Berry, the owner, skimmed the scraps—mostly solidified drops of batter from the fish—off the top of the oil he used for frying. When these had drained and cooled, they were either put in the waste bin or thrown into a cardboard box lined with white wrapping paper. The box was then transferred to the brick-built shed behind the shop which Berry used as a store and preparation room. It was built like a garage, with wide double doors and a concrete apron sloping down to a drain and then on for another few feet to the small street behind the shop. In warm weather the garage doors would be wide open, showing a stack of potatoes in sacks, jerricans of cooking oil, a vast ice box, a double sink, wooden cutting table and a rotary potato cleaner. This last had seen many years of service and would last many more because, according to Jack Berry, "there was nowt in it to go wrong and it cost nowt to run". This was a tribute to the sturdiness of the workmanship and the simplicity of design. It was, in essence, a drum the size of a dustbin, slung horizontally on an iron stand which carried the ends of a central axle. An extension of the axle at one end was fitted with a large cranking handle. This, turned by hand, rotated the drum—easy to do, even when half full of potatoes. The scraping and peeling was effected in much the same way as a domestic grater operates on a nutmeg or piece of cheese. The cylinder of the drum was perforated with close-set holes that had been driven in from outside to leave rough claws of metal standing proud inside. To lubricate the operation and to wash away mud and scraps of skin, the drum turned inside another half drum slung beneath it and filled with water.

Jack Berry had never seen any reason to exchange this highly satisfactory, reliable and economic piece of equipment for some new, more sophisticated and expensive equivalent. Particularly as he never seemed to be short of volunteers to turn the handle. Local ten- and twelve-year-old lads were quite capable of doing the work, and were always willing to do so for the obvious reward—a good big bag of hot chips fresh from the first frying, soused in vinegar and liberally sprinkled with salt.

Besides the lads, over the years, Joe Howlett had been accustomed to helping out when he was in the district, particularly in the preparation of the potatoes for lunch-time opening during term-time when the boys were in school. As an additional reward for long—if intermittent—service, Joe was allowed to help himself to the scraps from the box whenever they were there to be had, whether he had helped that day or not. His habit was to take them away to Burner's Wood, there to reheat them in a makeshift frying pan over a twig fire.

So Joe Howlett was fairly confident that what he had told Inspector Snell was correct. The tramp shuffled off down the High Street in the direction of Berry's shop, but before reaching it, turned off right down a side road and then left again to bring him to the back of the premises—the area with which he was so very familiar. The garage doors were open, and though there was no sign of Berry himself, there was the box of scraps in its usual place at the end of the preparation table. Joe, as had always been his custom, entered the premises, keeping his eyes open for a decent bit of paper or a plastic bag in which to wrap the scraps.

"Hey, you! What do you want in here?"

It was a heavy, unpleasant voice, but undoubtedly that of a woman. Though less refined than the voice that had berated him in the court, it was of the same timbre and reminded him strongly of Miss Foulger.

Joe looked up. Standing in the doorway at the back of the garage—the common entrance to the house and shop premises—was a large woman so heavily built that her legs were splayed apart by the sheer volume of her thighs. Though her bust must have boasted a gargantuan measurement, it was almost indiscernible except as an upward continuation of her great belly over which a green and white cotton frock was stretched like a newly inflated hot air balloon. Howlett recognised her from years ago. She was Berry's daughter who no longer lived in Colesworth.

"Scraps," he muttered, half-pointing towards the cardboard box. "Mr Berry always lets me have some."

"You're not getting any today. He's not here. He's gone on holiday and I'm in charge. And I'm not having a mucky old tramp like you hanging round. Dirty old ragamuffin! Get out of here before I turn the hose on you."

"The scraps . . ."

She took a pace towards the stand-pipe on the wall, her man-sized gumboots clopping ominously on the wet floor. "Out, you dirty old bastard! I hated the sight of you even when I was a kid. How my dad could ever let you . . ." She stooped to pick up the nozzle of the hose. With the business end pointed at Joe, and one pudgy hand on the tap top, she screamed: "I'll not tell you again."

Joe turned away. Evidently too slowly, too reluctantly for the bully girl. As he started to shamble off, a jet of water hit him between the shoulder blades. It was not powerful enough to knock him off his feet, but there was enough volume to wet the back of his clothes, his hair and his belongings. The tin containing the tea bags and sugar Watson had given him was half full of water, the contents completely ruined.

When he reached the pavement, with the wall for shelter, he turned. "Fat bitch," he yelled at her. "You ought to be in a sideshow." He dodged behind the wall as another jet of water hit

18

the brickwork. Then he again peered round the corner. "If they could find a tent big enough."

He mooched on, breathing imprecations against all women. As he went, he mumbled to himself, mouthing curses which covered Miss Foulger and Berry's daughter indiscriminately. For a normally mild-mannered man, he was very angry indeed, and not only with the two women, but with himself for being powerless to do anything to redress his grievances. Like a child he wanted revenge—to make them sorry for the way they had treated him.

It was in this frame of mind that he continued his way. He would now have to break into the pound note the inspector had given him. He would buy a loaf and then go to the kitchen door of the Albatross Hotel. On more than one occasion he had been given there the scooped-out rind of a Stilton with enough cheese left adhering to it to last him for days. But even the thought of this prospect did nothing to cool Joe's temper and his desire for revenge.

Inspector Snell reached the police station just as Sergeant Watson was about to leave the desk to have lunch in the canteen.

"I'd like a word with you, Tom. Private. In my office."

"Now, sir?"

"Yes, please. Come through."

Snell's office led off a corridor behind the desk space. It was the usual spartan place. All the furniture, with the exception of the filing cabinets, had been given a hurried coat of yellow varnish several decades earlier. The walls, however, had been newly colour-washed in duck-egg blue and a piece of chestnut coloured broadloom occupied two-thirds of the floor. The visitor's chair was an old carver, still yellow as to woodwork, but with a brown rexine seat that was a near-match for the carpet. Snell signalled to Watson to take this chair while he himself took off his uniform jacket and put it on a hanger in a cupboard.

"This is man to man, Tom," said Snell as he took his own chair. "Private, personal and off-the-record."

"Personal?"

Snell nodded.

"That sounds serious."

"There may be nothing in it, and I don't really know how to begin. The point is, Tom, I'm poking my nose into your business. My only excuse for doing so is that we're old mates, and I feel I would be letting you down if I were to keep quiet."

"I reckon we understand each other well enough to talk plain when we've got to, Roy."

"I'm pleased you see it like that, Tom, because it's . . . hell, man, it's like this. You know we had those three young villains, Boyce, Lawson and Mobb in court this morning."

"Of course I know. I also know they got away with it."

"And you know we were pretty sure they'd done four or five jobs before this last one?"

"I'm the desk-sergeant round here," said Watson drily. Then he changed his tone. "But you couldn't mention the other jobs."

"No. But before the hearing we did try to tie them in. We made a lot of enquiries, as you know, but we had no luck or not enough time."

Watson nodded to show he appreciated the point.

Snell continued. "During the enquiries we talked to a lot of informants."

"Naturally."

"One of mine—one I trust, otherwise I wouldn't be passing on what was said—told me something I think you ought to hear."

"What?"

"It's your Pam, Tom. I was told she has been seen running about with those three yobbos. Pam and Rosie Sewell."

There was a long moment of silence before Watson asked: "You're sure of this, Roy?"

"In so far as I trust my informant, yes."

"Who is he, your informant?"

"I'm not telling you that, Tom. You know the game."

"All right, all right! But my Pam . . . with those three? Why, they're . . . they're devils double-dipped."

"That's putting it mildly. So I reckon you ought to find out if it's true, Tom, and if so, put a stop to it before it goes too far."

"You're not suggesting my lass had anything to do with those break-ins?"

"No, definitely not. All I'm saying is that Pam's a pretty girl and would attract those three like a jar of honey does wasps. Those three particular wasps are a bit older than Pam . . ."

"What's that got to do with it?"

"I was just going to say your girl is probably impressionable and thinks it's smart to be seen with them at discos and the youth club. Nothing more than that. But I thought you'd want to do something about it before Pam really *does* get involved. As for Rosie Sewell . . . well, I know very little about her."

"Empty-headed little piece," murmured Watson abstractedly, obviously uninterested in Rosie. "She'd not lead my Pam astray . . ." He looked up. "Roy, this is a hell of a shock."

"Of course it is. I know what you and your missus think of the girl. That's why I've told you."

"Yes, thanks. This'll upset her mother. Knock her backwards."

"Does Freda have to know? Why don't you go home now and have a word with Pam? If there's nothing in the story . . ."

"I'm on duty, Roy."

"Forget the duty. Go home and see your daughter. How long is it since you've really seen anything of her?"

Watson shook his head. "By the time I get home she's usually gone out." He grimaced. "A copper can't always be there when he should be."

"I know. It's the big drawback of the job. That's why I say go home now and sort it out."

"I'll come back . . ."

"Tonight. Take the half-shift. I was going to have to find somebody. If you could do eight till two . . ."

The sergeant got to his feet. "Thanks, Roy. I know how difficult this must have been for you."

"I'm hoping it will turn out to be nothing. And, Tom, take it easy on the girl. Just because you think the light shines out of her is no reason to let worry carry you over the top."

"I'll remember. But when I think of those three yobs . . ."

Watson left the station and caught a bus for a free ride along the main road. He stood on the conductor's platform, paying little attention to anybody or anything but his own thoughts. But he did just notice Joe Howlett going into a baker's shop.

"What are you doing home, Tom?" asked Freda Watson in surprise.

"Changed duties, love. We're a bit pushed because of holidays so I said I'd do a half-shift tonight if I could have this nice sunny afternoon off to do a bit in the garden."

"Oh, I see. Do you want something to eat?"

"Have you had yours?"

"Half an hour since. Pam wants to go to the baths."

"In that case I'll have a sandwich and a can of beer. I'll just go up and change."

"Pam's upstairs."

"I don't need telling. This house will shake to bits one of these days. How these kids manage to stand the noise! I'll bet the roof joists are bouncing."

"I've asked her to turn it down a bit."

"I'll see what I can do."

Watson knocked on the door of his daughter's room and entered. It was obvious she had not heard the knock. She lay on her back on the bed, seemingly oblivious to everything but the beat, beat, beat of the record player. Watson had to move in close to stand above her, within her immediate vision, before she noticed him.

"Turn it down a bit, love," he shouted.

She sat up, noticeably put-out by the request, and lowered the volume of the player beside the bed to about half its former power.

"What do you want, dad? Shouldn't you be at work?"

Watson undid his tunic and loosened his tie, to give the impression that this was a normal, casual visit.

"Changed shifts, love. Mum tells me you're going swimming."

"I am."

"When?"

"What is this, dad? A cross-examination?"

He sat on the side of the bed and gestured towards the record player.

"I suppose that means you want me to turn it off?" she asked.

22

"It would help."

She switched off. In the blessed silence she looked at her father. "Satisfied?"

Watson pretended to ignore the unaccustomed enmity in her tone; made no comment about the unprecedented impertinence. "Not entirely. I want to talk to you."

"What about?"

Watson wondered whether it was his imagination seeing things that weren't there, or whether a hint of defensive fear had shown in his daughter's eyes. He disliked the way, too, in which she had suddenly tensed her body. He remembered Snell's advice and decided to play it gently.

"Who are you going swimming with?"

"Coral."

"Coral? You mean Carol, don't you? Carol Gilbert?"

"She's decided she'd prefer to be called Coral."

"Why? Because she thinks she looks like Marilyn Monroe?"

"Yes."

"Tell her Marilyn Monroe didn't have knock-knees."

"They don't show under skirts."

"They will at the swimming baths, unless she's going to wear those frilly Victorian pantaloons."

Pam didn't reply. She sat leaning against the bed head, picking at the cover and not looking at her father.

"Who else is going? Rosie Sewell?"

"P'raps."

"Boyfriends? Three young seventeen-year-olds like you must have boyfriends these days, I reckon."

She glanced at him, as if waiting watchfully for what was to come next. They sat looking at each other for another moment or two. Then he got to his feet.

"When I say that three good-looking girls like you, Rosie and Carol . . . er . . . Coral, must have boyfriends, love, I mean decent lads. Not yobbos like those three who used to go to your school and we had up in court today—Boyce, Lawson and Mobb."

She suddenly flared up at him.

"You've been spying on me!"

23

"You know I'd never do that, Pam," he replied quietly.

"Do I? You're the fuzz, aren't you?" Her voice was becoming hysterical in its accusation.

"I'm the fuzz all right. But I haven't been spying on you."

"Somebody must have."

"What makes you say that?"

"You talking about Norm, Eric and Ted like that."

"Norm, Eric and Ted?" He again remembered Snell's advice, and strove to keep calm. "That's what they're called, is it?"

"Yes." She sneered the names. "Boyce, Lawson and Mobb! They're not people to the fuzz, are they? Just . . . just things."

"Hold it, hold it, love! What are you trying to tell me? That you know those three? That they're friends of yours? That you actually go about with them?"

"Yes, I do. And you know I do, else you wouldn't be up here smarming away pretending you didn't know."

His voice changed. "I didn't know," he said severely. "Not until half an hour ago. Those lads have been investigated—what they do, where they go, and who they go with. What do you think I felt like when I heard you and Rosie Sewell mentioned in connection with those three by one of my colleagues? That's how I got to know, but I couldn't really believe it."

"Why not?"

"Because you're a decent girl. A good kid. That's why not."

"I'm not a kid. And you did believe it, else you wouldn't be here."

"I had to come to make sure the report was wrong."

"Well it wasn't."

Mrs Watson appeared in the doorway. "What's going on here? I could hear your voices . . ." She looked from daughter to husband. "What's going on, Tom?"

"I'll tell you downstairs." He turned to his daughter. "Rosie Sewell and Carol Gilbert can do as they like, but you are to stop having anything to do with those three villains. If I hear another whisper of you being with them there'll be trouble. Serious trouble. That's all I'm going to say about it, but see you do as you're told."

As Watson followed his wife downstairs he distinctly heard the shouted words: "Go to hell, fuzz."

Freda said: "Have your beer and sandwiches and tell me what all this is about, Tom. You've got me really worried."

"There's no need to be worried now, love. I'm sure she'll see sense."

"What about?"

Watson told her what he knew. He finished by saying: "Don't harrass her about it, Freda, but try and find out what you can and try to discourage her from seeing those lads. If we don't manage it . . ."

"She'll be in court the next thing we know?"

"She'll be lucky if that's all it is. What I'm afraid of is that those three yobs will make a point of involving Pam in some villainy, knowing she's a police-sergeant's daughter."

"Why?"

"They're probably under the impression that it would get us off their backs. Well, it wouldn't. And then there's this business of going into Burner's Wood. I don't like it."

Neither did his wife, and said so fearfully. Eventually she asked: "Are you really going to do the garden, Tom?"

"Might as well. Work some of this anger out of my system."

"In that case, after you've changed and got started, I'll try and have a word with Pam. You never know . . ."

"Never know what, love?"

"They could have set her against the police. All policemen."

"Including me, by the sound of it."

"So perhaps she'll listen to me better than you."

Watson nodded glumly. It was apparent to Freda how much this thought hurt him. He had always adored Pam and, until recently, father and daughter had been great friends. In the past few weeks, Mrs Watson had attributed the change in the girl's attitude simply to her growing up: to the modern disease that claims so many teenagers as victims of a malaise which was unheard of in her own day—the generation gap.

"You could be right, love. Try and make her see sense." Watson got heavily to his feet to go upstairs once again to change.

Chapter 2

THAT NIGHT, WATSON was again behind the desk at the Coles-worth station—alone in an apparently deserted building—when the radio call came. He glanced automatically at the clock so that he could log the call. Twenty past ten.

It was Constable Sutcliffe.

"Sarge, I've got young Boyce here."

"Got? What do you mean? Arrested him, have you?"

"No, Sarge, he's drunk."

"How drunk?"

"As a fiddler's bitch, Sarge. I found him sprawled on the pave-ment, stinking of booze. I've tried to get him on his feet but he can't stand. I'm having to hold him up."

"You want to bring him in?"

"I'll have to, Sarge, for his own safety. There's no charge as far as I can tell, but he'll have to sleep it off, won't he?"

"I suppose so. I'll send a car. Where are you?"

"Halfway down Callandar Street, outside Burton's."

"Right. Any sign of his two mates, Lawson and Mobb?"

"No, Sarge. Hurry it up, please, he's getting heavy."

"Put him down, lad. There'll be a car there in a couple of minutes."

Watson radioed instructions to the nearest car and turned back to the desk to make his notes. It was a warm night late in July and his shirt was damp with sweat. Boyce! Watson clamped his jaws in distaste as he wrote the name in the incident book.

It was only the third entry he had made since coming on duty. The first had been a complaint from Miss Foulger. Had his mind not been so occupied with his daughter and her friendship with the young man who was about to be brought in—according to Sutcliffe—dead drunk, he would have thought it a surprising coincidence that the magistrate who had heard the Boyce case and the accused himself should both appear so close together in the book. Miss Foulger, it appeared, was something of a home wine maker. Her cottage on the outskirts of Colesworth boasted a small brick outhouse—a former laundry—where she now housed a deep-freeze cabinet and her wine-making equipment. During her absence from home somebody had entered the outhouse and broken six bottles of wine which she had siphoned off before leaving for court that morning. They had been left standing on a bench, from which they had been knocked to break on the stone floor, leaving the place strewn with broken glass swimming in white wine. With so little damage done, Watson might well have ignored the report, but because Miss Foulger was Chairman of the bench, he had sent a constable to get a statement which would appear, no doubt, in the morning.

The second complaint had come from a Mrs Edna Corby who had explained that she was the daughter of Jack Berry, owner of the nearby fish and chip shop. She was looking after the shop for her father, and had left the gumboots she wore when hosing down the preparation shed standing beside the sink. She had also, it appeared, been unwise enough to leave the doors of the shed open, thereby giving somebody the opportunity to sneak in unseen and deposit in her boots a liberal helping of—to use her own words—dog muck. She had inserted her bare feet into the boots before fully appreciating the presence of their unpleasant contents. Mrs Corby had expressed herself as highly incensed by this incident and demanded to know what the police intended to do about apprehending and then jailing the practical joker. Watson hadn't told her that he proposed to do precisely nothing, but that is exactly what he did, apart from logging the complaint.

Ten minutes after the call from Sutcliffe, the constable and the driver of the car, P.C. Younghouse, were carrying Boyce into the station.

"Completely blotto, Sarge," said Younghouse. "And he stinks of booze."

"I said it first," grunted Sutcliffe, releasing a limp arm from round his neck.

"Don't dump him there," ordered Watson. "Straight into number three cell with him. It's open. Lay him down to sleep it off and see he hasn't got any of our blankets near him. I don't want him puking over everything we've got."

"Who's jailer tonight, Sarge?"

"There isn't one. We haven't got the staff, have we? Only for Friday and Saturday nights."

"Do we lock the cell?" asked Younghouse.

"I'll be there in a minute."

"To take his bovver boots off, Sarge?"

"You can do that, lad. Go on, take him away."

Boyce was plonked unceremoniously on the bare cot. Younghouse emptied the pockets of the tight jeans, while Sutcliffe took off the heavy, rubber-soled boots.

"Are you sure we shouldn't give him a blanket, Sarge? He's only got a thin T-shirt up top."

"I've got eyes in my head, lad. No blanket. Right, let's see what he's got? Two quid in notes, seventy-four pence in coin . . . here, what's he doing with this?"

"It's a cork, Sarge—or, rather, it's one of those modern plastic stoppers some bottles have these days. He probably picked it up in the pub."

"Like a magpie. Picks up anything that takes his eye."

"Are you going to book him, Sarge?"

"We'll see in the morning. If there are any reports about some young yob misbehaving . . ." They left the cell and locked the door behind them. Younghouse drove off in his car to resume his patrol. Watson said to Sutcliffe: "You might as well take your break now. It's getting on for eleven. Come and see me before you go, though, because I'll need your report."

As Sutcliffe went for his supper, Watson completed the book entries, carefully timing each entry until the final one—*Cell 3 locked on occupant at 22.53. No charges preferred.*

A minute or two before half past eleven, Sutcliffe reappeared, carrying a cup of tea. "Not bad pie and chips tonight, Sarge."

"Get writing," said Watson, ignoring the gastronomic comment. "How you found him. The lot."

"Just for a drunk, Sarge? If you're not going to charge him . . ."

"Do it, lad."

Sutcliffe sighed. He would rather be out on the beat than doing paperwork on a hot summer's night, especially for a young drunk who would be let go in the morning. He supposed Watson was playing it safe with Boyce, in case there had been some incident not yet reported but which could implicate the youth and lead to a charge. He, Watson and Snell would all like to nail Boyce. So, Sutcliffe supposed, Watson wanted chapter and verse in case the chance came to get back on the villain who had made a monkey out of the Colesworth police for so long.

At last Sutcliffe handed over his report. "It's all there, Sarge."

"Right. Go down and make sure Boyce is all there, too, lad."

"He couldn't have broken out of a doll's house in his state, Sarge."

"Never mind that. Look in on him for a routine check and log it for midnight."

"Why all the bother, Sarge?"

Watson frowned. "We're not going to put a foot wrong with this one this time, Sutcliffe. But it needn't concern you. Get on with it."

Sutcliffe departed slowly down the corridor that led to the cells. His mind was not on the man he had been sent to visit. He was thinking that, despite the heat, he had better put on a tunic for the rest of his patrol. It could be bloody cold in the small hours even in the hottest spell. When he arrived outside number three, he peered disinterestedly through the spy hole. For a moment or two he stood there and then he turned and legged it back in a hurry.

"Okay is he?"

"I think I'd better have the keys, Sarge."

The suggestion caused Watson to stare for a moment and then to reach hurriedly under the counter for the large ring of jailer's keys.

"What's up, lad?"

"Maybe nothing, Sarge, but I honestly don't like the look of him."

"I'll come."

They went together. Watson, after a quick look through the spy hole, hurried noticeably in selecting the right key and unlocking the door.

The body was sprawled on the cot much as it had been when first dumped. But whereas then there had been obvious and, indeed, noisy breathing, now there was only a stillness—Boyce was a limp and silent mass from which all semblance of life had, apparently, passed.

His face puckered by worry frowns and grimacing with distaste at the smell, Watson bent over the body. He tried to detect breathing at the dropped-open mouth and felt for pulses at neck and wrist. When he straightened up, his face was solemn-grey and glistening with sweat.

"He's gone, lad. Lock up and stay around. I'll get Dr Scovell and Mr Snell on the blower."

When Sutcliffe rejoined Watson at the desk, the sergeant was speaking to the inspector at his home.

". . . the doctor says he'll be here immediately. Yes, I'll keep Sutcliffe here until you arrive. No, sir, nobody went into him after the cell was locked. We put him in at ten thirty-five and left him soon after a quarter to eleven. Sutcliffe made the midnight inspection—a few minutes early, that was—and that's when . . . yes, sir, all logged."

Watson put the phone down. "Get some coffee up here, lad. We're going to need some sustenance before this party's over."

Dr Rex Scovell had been a police surgeon for more than a decade. He knew what to do and how to do it in cases of sudden and unexpected death. What he was equally sure of was that many of the policemen he had to work with on these occasions—particularly the young ones—regarded much of what he did as so much mumbo-jumbo. So, whenever possible, Scovell sought to dispel the mystique of his profession by turning his examinations into illustrated lectures for the benefit of his audience. A well-lit police cell seemed an appropriate place with Watson an appropriate audience. Sutcliffe had been left to man the desk.

"The first thing," said Scovell, who had dressed so hurriedly that, though he wore a pair of grey slacks, he still had on a pyjama jacket, the collar of which showed above the thin sweater he had pulled on over it, "the first thing, Sergeant Watson, and the most important, is to make sure that the chap is well and truly dead."

"I made pretty sure, sir," said Watson as Scovell knelt beside the body.

"I'm sure you did, but there have been times when so-called corpses have revived on mortuary slabs. Caused a few red faces in my trade. Remember that people suffering from hypothermia or who have been electrocuted and, sometimes, those who have been poisoned are the ones likely to start groaning or moving after they have been taken for dead."

"I see, sir."

"Vital functions," murmured Scovell, using his stethoscope and fingers to search for signs of life. "Breathing and heart-beat irreversibly ceased, but we must test him for quite a few minutes, not just cursorily. Auscultation—using the stethoscope—for heart or breath sounds is best. The old trick of using a feather or a mirror is not as reliable. Now . . ." he put down the stethoscope, ". . . the eyes." He took an ophthalmoscope from his bag. As he screwed his face up and lifted one of Boyce's eyelids, he continued: ". . . You can often confirm that the blood has stopped flowing by looking . . . yes . . . there are signs of the collapse of the columns of blood in the retinal vessels."

He looked up. "That's virtually it, Sergeant. Together with pallor of the skin and flaccidity of the muscles." He lifted one arm and let it fall to prove his point. "Now I suppose I'd better take a few temperature readings, but my guess is they'll tell us nothing we don't know. A warm night like this and so soon after death . . . no cooling, no rigor . . . you know when he died, don't you? Between what? Eleven and a quarter to twelve?"

"We left him about a quarter to eleven, sir. He was alive then, but dead drunk."

"Yes, he'd had some drink without a doubt. And when exactly did you find him dead?"

"A few minutes before twelve. Constable Sutcliffe came to do the midnight routine visit a bit early, like."

Scovell got to his feet. "Well, Sergeant, I'm afraid this is a case for the coroner. It comes under the headings of Death in Suspicious Circumstances and Being Summoned by the Police."

Watson looked a worried man. He was about to reply to Scovell when Inspector Snell, fully uniformed, hurried in.

"You've got a bit of a problem on your hands here, Roy," said the doctor.

"Death in police custody, you mean?"

"That's right. I've got to send a Med A to the coroner on about half-a-dozen counts—unexpected death, unexplained death, haven't attended deceased within fourteen days, alcoholism, perhaps poisoning, death in legal custody and, according to how you instruct me, there could be crime or suspected crime."

"Crime? He died of drink, didn't he?"

Scovell shook his head in doubt. "I can't say for sure, yet. It's obvious, I agree, that he had been drinking, and this cell stinks like a brewery to prove it. But have you noticed anything missing?"

"Yes," mumbled Watson. "He hasn't puked."

"Right. Your average drunk throws up. Boyce didn't."

"Meaning?" demanded Snell.

"There's a possibility that though he had been drinking he hadn't got to the stage of being drunk."

"But he was lying out on a pavement, doctor. Incapable, according to Sutcliffe."

"That could well be. But not through being incapable because of drink if we take the absence of vomit into account. We'll have to ask the constable if he vomited on the pavement, of course, or in the car on the way here."

"Not in the car, he didn't," said Watson firmly, "or I'd have heard about it."

"We'll ask Sutcliffe," said Snell. "What I want to know is, if it wasn't drink, what did he die of, Rex?"

Scovell said: "What are you asking me to do, Roy? Simply to establish that the man is dead? Or are you proposing to ask me to make a more detailed examination because you intend to investigate the death as suspicious?"

"The latter. I've no choice."

"Fair enough. I've been careful not to touch or destroy anything. I've heard the statements of Watson and Sutcliffe concerning why Boyce was brought in. I've checked time of death. I've checked there are no obvious marks or injuries and noted the state of the clothing. I've searched for, and failed to find bloodstains, cups, bottles, syringes, weapons, drugs, tablets . . . the lot. All I've got to do now is to make a quick sketch of the position of the body, check that the identity of the chap is correct and get his full name from you. After that, I'll get it all down on paper—in your office, if you don't mind. I'll report to the coroner immediately. He'll arrange for the body to be moved for autopsy. He'll get Haywood to do it, I expect. And he'll order the full works." He glanced at Watson. "Sorry, old chap, but that's how it will be. I can't give you any grain of comfort at this stage because quite honestly I don't know how young Boyce died. I'm just not familiar with what appears to have happened here and, without a post-mortem, I don't think any doctor could give a firm opinion. So, shall we go to the office?"

Sutcliffe confirmed there had been no signs of vomit in the street where he had found Boyce. Whilst waiting for the car he had made a point—after putting Boyce back on the pavement—of searching the area round the body for . . . well, for weapons or articles that could have been nicked or bottles of drink.

As soon as Snell and Scovell had left them, Watson said: "There's going to be hell to pay over this, lad. Why the devil it had to be you that found him and me that was on the desk, I don't know. But I'll tell you, young Sutcliffe, before long we're going to wish we'd never heard the name of Norman Boyce."

The news of Boyce's strange death broke dramatically the next morning.

Bennett, the *Colesworth Gazette* crime reporter who had approached Snell in the corridor outside the courtroom the previous morning, had made a habit of dropping into the police station on his way to the office each day. There he was usually courteously received and given any snippets of news that the police could afford to let him have—crashes, fires, drownings and the rest.

In the seven or eight years of his experience as a crime reporter, Bennett had developed a hide of leather and antennae so sensitive that they could log the slightest change from normal in the atmosphere at the police station. The reception he received that morning screamed aloud that something out of the ordinary had happened overnight. Other observations helped to reinforce the impression. Bennett had noted that standing outside the station were the cars—both known to him—of the Divisional Chief Superintendent and of the Detective Chief Superintendent. Both were comparatively rare visitors, and for them both to be at Colesworth together, at so early an hour, argued that something out of the ordinary was afoot. Inside the station, the sight of Sergeant Tom Watson still unshaven at nine o'clock argued a situation serious enough to transcend routine discipline.

Once put on the trail by these pointers, Bennett was not to be headed off. The fact that nobody in the station would tell him anything only served to confirm his belief that he had stumbled across a big story. From then on he only had to try his other sources—the hospital, fire brigade, ambulance service and the like. It was the morgue attendant—who charged a fiver for the information—who produced the goods. The body of a youth had come in early from the nick. The name tag identified the corpse as that of Norman Boyce. The pathologist, Professor Haywood, who held the chair of Forensic Medicine at Aveling College, had sent word to say that he proposed to start the autopsy at eleven o'clock that morning.

Norman Boyce! Bennett had heard the case in the Magistrates' Court and he still remembered that Snell had not been exactly co-operative later, in the corridor. Perhaps this could be Bennett's chance to make Snell pay for shrugging off the press.

Bennett remembered the other two youths who had been charged with Boyce. It didn't take him long to find Lawson and Mobb and—as he had expected—found them to be mines of information.

Sure, Boyce had been in a pub last night, but he'd only had a couple of halves. It took more than that to make Norman Boyce drunk. He'd been all right when they had last seen him, and they reckoned the fuzz had picked him up because they had a down on all three of them and were disappointed that the court had not jailed them.

This seemed a fair enough assumption to Bennett who had overheard Sutcliffe's angry reaction to the outcome of the court case. Sutcliffe, after all, had vowed to "bang-up" the trio "no matter what".

Girlfriends? Yes, Norman Boyce had a girlfriend. Pam Watson —Sergeant Watson's daughter. Did Dad approve of the relationship? Lawson and Mobb didn't think Dad even knew about it, but they reckoned one thing was sure and that was that when Dad did get to know there'd be hell to pay.

Bennett had left them with a pound note apiece and had then hurried to Watson's house to ask Pam what she had to say about her boyfriend's death in police custody.

As a result of Bennett's exertions, the *Colesworth Gazette* put out a Special that morning—something it hadn't done since Coronation Day. According to the front page article, Pam Watson, on hearing from Bennett that Boyce had died overnight in a police cell, had become hysterical and shouted over and over again that her father had killed him because he disapproved of the relationship and because she, Pam, was expecting Boyce's child.

There followed a paragraph about how Watson should not have been on duty that night, thereby hinting that there was something not only mysterious but sinister about the sergeant's presence in the police station when Boyce was brought in. This mystery was heightened, claimed Bennett, by the fact that the arresting officer, Constable Sutcliffe, should not have been on duty either. And he went on to say how he himself had overheard Sutcliffe's voiced intention of seeing that Boyce and his two companions got what was coming to them, after they had been let off by the magistrates.

It was all there, in black and white. The editor of the *Gazette* had really had no choice but to print it. Bennett, who was also a stringer for the London evening press, had phoned the story through and was delighted to hear that not only did the early editions feature it, but also that the lunchtime news broadcasts carried it.

There were those in the Colesworth police station who did not share Bennett's pleasure in these revelations.

Detective Chief Superintendent Crewkerne, and Chief Superintendent Warne, the two whose cars had been noticed and identified by Bennett, had come to Colesworth as soon as they had learned of Boyce's death. They had first conferred with Inspector Snell, then they had interviewed Watson and Sutcliffe separately. After that they had questioned Constable Younghouse and then inspected the incident ledger, generally treating the affair in a level-headed way, but regarding it nonetheless as a serious and deplorable case of unfortunate death while in legal custody.

There was no reason to take any other course. Dr Scovell's report stated clearly enough that there were no marks of violence on the body and certainly nobody had treated Boyce, while still alive, in any way more harshly than the unceremonious fashion of his transportation to the cell demanded. It was only after the *Gazette* Special hit the streets and the Chief Constable had heard a lunchtime news bulletin that the enquiry began to take on a different aspect.

The Chief Constable himself arrived at Colesworth before two o'clock. Watson was interviewed again and denied that he knew his daughter to be pregnant, let alone that Boyce was the father of the child. A detective was sent to interview Pamela Watson who agreed she might have said something like Bennett's report, but only because she assumed her father knew her to be pregnant. The reason for such an assumption was the fact that she had confessed her state to her mother during their talk the previous afternoon and had supposed that her mother had passed the news on to her father. Mrs Watson denied telling her husband because Pam herself had begged her not to.

Snell was recalled and told the group of senior officers that he had come to hear of Pam's involvement with Boyce and why he had informed Sergeant Watson of the involvement. He was careful not to reveal the source of his information, and the other officers present had been too preoccupied to think of asking him to do so, even had they been prepared to demand a name. Snell also explained how it was that Watson and Sutcliffe came to be on night duty.

36

Sutcliffe, on his second appearance, confessed that in the heat of the moment, outside the court, he had said to a colleague that he intended to make sure that Boyce, Lawson and Mobb got their just deserts.

It all sounded terribly thin this second time round and the D.C.S. looked glum as he spoke to the Chief Constable. "I don't like to suggest this, but it's beginning to look as though you'll have to suspend Watson and Sutcliffe."

"Why?" asked the uniformed chief superintendent, determined to put up some sort of defence for his own men.

"So that we can set up an official enquiry."

"Enquiry into what?"

"Into a death while in police custody and also into the less-than-satisfactory story that Watson and Sutcliffe have told."

The Chief Constable, who had listened to all that had been said, but had contributed little himself, now spoke. "Less-than-satisfactory to whom? To us? Or by the standards set by a local news reporter?"

"To test the story for ourselves, sir."

"But to institute an enquiry, we must have adequate cause. On what grounds will you base your enquiry should I agree to it?"

The D.C.S. frowned. "I said I didn't like it. But what Watson's daughter said is enough."

"That her father knew of her condition?"

"Yes."

"You are willing to accept the hysterical ravings of a teenage girl as reported in a newspaper before the word of her father—a trusted and able man—and to crucify him on that account? Because, believe me, an enquiry such as you suggest would crucify him."

"If we don't, the public will."

The Chief Constable shook his head. "If Watson is in the clear, he will ride the newspaper reports, but if he is pilloried by his own colleagues it will finish him."

D.C.S. Crewkerne acknowledged the truth of this, but asked: "What *are* we going to do then? Those bloody newshounds will demand something, and enquiries such as I've suggested are the only moves that will satisfy them."

"I shall decide when I know how Boyce died. The medical reports confirm that our men did not use violence. How do you suggest they could have murdered him?"

"Murdered?"

"What else would it be if it were not death from some sort of natural causes?"

"I never mentioned murder."

"Then please tell me, Aubrey, why you wish to conduct an enquiry into the actions of Watson and Sutcliffe."

The D.C.S. shook his head glumly. "There'll be questions asked," he forecast, "and I would like us to be in a position to answer them."

"Agreed. But not at the expense of two of our men against whom—so far, at least—there is no evidence."

The uniform-branch superintendent applauded this, and was in the middle of suggesting to Crewkerne that statements should be taken and filed, unofficially, against the chance of storms ahead, when the phone rang. The Chief Constable was asked if he would take a call from Professor Haywood, the pathologist.

The C.C. took over the phone and announced himself.

"Ah! Just the chap," said Haywood, a still youthful man with a still youthful turn of phrase. "I expect you've been getting a bit twitchy about this Boyce character, in view of the bad press you're getting."

"It is disturbing, Professor," admitted the C.C.

"Then I'm glad to be able to set your mind at rest—in part, at least. The lad died of a fatal thrombocytopenia."

"What's that in layman's words?"

"It's what we in the trade call a blood dyscrasia. Dyscrasia simply means disorder."

"So he died of a blood disorder?"

"That's the strength of it. And it lets out your officers in the station last night, despite the insinuations in the *Gazette*."

"You are absolutely sure of that? I mean, I can count on it?"

"There was no way they could have induced a blood disorder in Boyce in the time he was in their hands, short of injecting him with massive doses of some toxic material."

"Which they didn't?"

"Nary an injection mark on him. He may have been a young tearaway, but he wasn't on the needle, praise be."

"And they couldn't have fed him some substance by mouth?"

"I think not."

"Only think?"

"I can discover no signs of forcible feeding, and it would have to be forcible to get something down a chap who is *stinko profundo*. There would be marks or stains round the mouth—that sort of thing—and there weren't any. So I think they didn't feed him anything unless they've perfected a means of administration unknown to the medical world. But the time factor works here, too. You could feed a quick acting poison to a man and kill him off in less than an hour and a half, but I can't think of anything that would cause so total a blood disorder as to kill him in that time. And that, in my opinion, exonerates your chaps."

"Thank you for that. Now about this disorder. What was it?"

"A massive decrease in the number of blood platelets."

"So he could have died at any time."

"No, no! Hold your horses, Chief Constable. I rang you to set your mind at rest over your two officers who are under a cloud. But don't run away with the idea that your job is over. That lad was killed by a toxic substance. In other words, he was poisoned earlier in the day."

"What by?"

"I don't know the substance yet. There are scads of tests to be done. What I can tell you is that Boyce could not have lived for a full day in the state he was in. I also know that fatal blood dyscrasias can occur suddenly. But that is a relative term, meaning at the minimum a period of . . . well, certainly not within the short time he was in police custody."

"Any ideas at all, Professor?"

"As to exactly when he took the stuff? Not really. Your people say that when he was picked up he was well and truly sloshed, which I think he was. But his friends say he only had two halves of beer when he was with them last night. If that's true, then he had something else to drink elsewhere or—and this could be the right answer—at the time your people found him he may have been under the influence, not of drink exclusively, but also of some of the nasties that can accompany thrombocytopenia."

"Could those nasties, as you call them, appear like the effects of drunkenness to the layman?"

"In the street at night in a character smelling of booze? Oh, yes. Your chaps aren't doctors. In fact, I think most doctors would have been fooled at the outset. So I don't think your officers could be expected to know what was wrong. I've heard from the police surgeon that they monitored him in the accepted way and, so far as I can make out, the only things out of the ordinary were that Boyce wasn't noisy, he didn't vomit and he wasn't actively unco-operative."

"Those things sometimes happen. Often, in fact."

"Quite. Well, now I've got your chaps off the hook for you, I'll get on with the job. There's a hell of a lot still left to do in the laboratory, and the coroner won't get his written report till it's completed."

"Thank you, Professor. I hope all of this will come out at the inquest so that the public will learn the truth."

"I'll do my best for you. But if I were you, Chief Constable, I'd get my sleuths on to discovering how this otherwise healthy young man came to be in the state that killed him. Quite frankly, I think you will have to work on the presumption that somebody poisoned him deliberately."

"Murder?"

"That's what I'd call it, but these days they water murder down and call it manslaughter or justifiable homicide or some such thing. But I'd begin to look into it if I were you because I'm positive my report is going to force the coroner to require you to do so. And, Chief Constable . . ."

"Yes?"

"Get a smart jack on to it, won't you? This is going to be tricky—technically tricky, I mean—and you're not going to clear your name completely unless you make a first class job of the investigation."

"Thank you."

"I just thought I'd mention it."

"When I said thank you, I really meant it. Both for the advice and the great help you've given me."

"In that case, so long. See you in court."

The Chief Constable repeated the gist of the conversation he had had with Haywood. It wasn't a difficult task because all of them present had gathered much of what had been said. The only bit the C.C. did not mention was the professor's final bit of advice about the advisability of making sure of success in the investigation which now faced them.

"Snell," said the C.C., "are Watson and Sutcliffe still on the premises?"

"Yes, sir."

"Go and put them out of their misery. But keep quiet about the poison. Just tell them he died of a blood disorder exacerbated by drink."

"Right, sir."

"And send them off. They've been on duty since eight o'clock last night and Watson, at least, has got trouble to sort out at home."

"Sir!"

After Snell had gone, the C.C. turned to the other two officers. "We've got a dog's dinner here," he said. "A lot of the mud that's already been thrown is going to stick. An unfortunate death while in police custody, which sounds as though it could be murder, is going to be quite a target for mudslingers."

"A murder committed before we were involved," reminded Warne.

"True. But I wonder how many worthy citizens are going to cock a knowing eye when we try to put that across?"

"It's a pound to a penny," grumbled Crewkerne, "that the local rag will be talking about a police cover-up by tomorrow night's edition."

The C.C. asked: "Do you honestly believe that, Aubrey? Even if they know that you are conducting an enquiry?"

The D.C.S. nodded. "We've had some. The police are a law

unto themselves! They investigate their own misdeeds and find themselves not guilty!"

"How can they say that," demanded Warne, "when they learn that the pathologist has cleared my men?"

"But he hasn't," said the D.C.S. "He has only cleared them for the one and a half hours during which Boyce was in the nick. What if our chaps got at him earlier?"

"Rubbish!"

"Maybe. But somebody is going to think of that and say we are using Haywood's report as a get-out. Particularly if we can't find whoever it was who fed the lad the poison."

The Chief Superintendent considered this for a moment or two and then turned to the C.C. "Is that how you see it, sir?"

"I'm afraid I do. However, I really believe that Aubrey and his men could and would find the culprit."

"Could and would?" asked Warne.

"I'm not prepared to give anybody the slightest chance to even hint at a whitewash in this Division. We are going to be seen to bare our breasts to the scrutiny of investigators other than our own immediate colleagues. In other words, we are not going to conduct our own enquiry. We're going to get somebody in from outside to do it. The only decision to be made is whether I invite the C.C. of another Division to arrange it or whether I ask the Yard to do it. I'd like your opinions, gentlemen, please."

"I'm quite easy, sir," said Warne. "I'll be happy with whichever you decide."

The D.C.S. was more deliberate.

"Horses for courses," he said firmly. "In a case like this it's best to choose the best man for the job."

The C.C. nodded his agreement. Crewkerne's words were almost a repetition of those used by Professor Haywood.

The D.C.S. continued: "If it was a case of fatal injury with a lot of routine work involved, I'd opt for a Crime Squad man from another Division. But this is not injury, it's medical—very tricky— and it's going to take a man with a track record in just such cases to do it properly." He looked squarely at the C.C. "In my opinion, sir, we should nominate the man we want."

"That sounds logical. Who had you in mind, Aubrey?"

"D.C.S. George Masters of the Yard. He's a specialist in this sort of case."

"Thank you both for your help and advice, and you, Aubrey, for your unquestioning agreement to call in somebody to do a job you could undoubtedly do yourself. I'll ring the Yard and ask for Masters. Let us hope he's free to help."

Chapter 3

MASTERS WAS FREE to help.

Though he and his team were not at the top of the list to answer outside calls for assistance, Anderson the A.C. (Crime) was very happy to accede to the Chief Constable's request to send a specialist team for a specialist job.

"Whoever decided to ask for Masters by name was a sensible chap," the A.C. said.

The C.C., at the other end of the phone, admitted that it had been the decision of his D.C.S.

"Who is your D.C.S.?"

"Crewkerne."

"Aubrey Crewkerne? He and I are of the same vintage. We were colleagues many moons ago, and he'll know Masters. Crewkerne was, I believe, a D.I. here when Masters joined us as a detective constable."

"Then we should have a happy team."

"More important, you'll have the best team. Now Chief Constable, please give me a brief rundown of your problem so that I don't have to send Masters out to you completely cold."

By the time the phoned report was finished it was after half past five. Anderson immediately rang through to Masters.

"George, there's an outside job for you."

"You know I'm not on standby, sir?"

"You've been asked for by name. Come up and hear all about it after you've warned Green and your sergeants."

"You mean we're to go this evening, sir?"

"'Fraid so, George. To Colesworth. It will take you the best part of a couple of hours to get there by road, and the Colesworth people are quite twitchy."

"That's where the cell-death occurred, isn't it?"

"The same."

"Then I can understand them being a little tense. Is that, in fact, the job we're wanted for?"

"How did you guess?"

"I'll join you in two minutes, sir."

Shortly after six they were on the road.

As so often happened, Masters briefed his team in the car as they went. When he had finished telling them what he had learned from Anderson, Detective Sergeant Berger, sitting in the front passenger seat, turned round to Masters in the opposite back and said: "As I see it, Chief, it all revolves round the question of whether the constable who picked up this villain Boyce should have done what he did or whether he should have called an ambulance and had him taken to hospital."

Before Masters could answer, D.C.I. Green, sitting as usual in the—to him—psychologically safer nearside rear seat, said: "It all revolves round that, does it, lad? Then in that case we might as well revolve this car and go home."

Berger looked astonished. "But if he'd been taken to hospital he'd either have been saved or he'd have died under medical care, and the local force wouldn't have been involved."

"The pathologist thinks it's murder, lad, and murder involves the police whether the victim dies in a cell, a hospital bed or a field of cowslips."

"I know that. But if Sergeant Watson and Constable Sutcliffe had acted differently . . ."

"They acted correctly," said Masters. "This is a grey area in police work to which nobody has yet found an answer."

"I don't follow you, Chief."

"Coppers," said Green, "can't shove drunks into hospitals unless the drunks are injured."

"Quite right, too," added Reed, keeping his eyes on the road while he joined in the conversation. As he overtook a small car, he continued: "I've seen some of it—we all have—on Saturday nights expecially. Swearing drunks, fighting mad, playing absolute havoc

45

with casualty departments in busy hospitals. You always have to get extra porters and cops off the street to restrain them. How the hell those young nurses stick it, I don't know. Vulgar language, puke all over the shop and the chance of a black eye or a broken nose for trying to help them. And those young doctors, too. I remember one of them once telling me that he had been on call for over a hundred hours that week, and he hadn't been paid as much for all that work as some of the drunks he was treating had spent on booze that one night.''

"That's common knowledge," said Green. "But the drunks wouldn't believe you, though, come to think of it, their wives might.''

"Alcoholism is growing worse and it's of great concern to the authorities," said Masters. "But the Home Affairs Committee that investigated deaths like this one—deaths in police custody, that is—reported that our way of dealing with drunks is as good as any, short of setting up special centres to which all drunks would be taken to sober up.''

"Sort of half hospital, half nick?" asked Green. "At the public's expense, I suppose?''

"The do-gooders have suggested them. Meanwhile, we compromise. We ignore drunks that are still on their feet. We take in those that are completely blotto or incapable of taking care of themselves, and we send the injured ones to hospital. That is our system, and I can't see that Sutcliffe and Watson were at fault in any way, particularly as the pathologist has reported that there are no marks of violence on the corpse.''

"So you'll ignore all this business about Boyce getting Watson's daughter pregnant?''

"I don't think I can say that at this stage. That fact may be relevant to discovering the how, the why and the who of Boyce's poisoning. But, equally, it could be just as much of a distraction in the way of getting at the real reason or motive for his death.''

"That's simplified that," said Green airily. "Let's hope the rest comes as easily.''

Masters started to fill his pipe. "You're a humbug, Bill.''

"What's that supposed to mean?''

46

"A gob-stopper," said Reed and then went on hurriedly, "After all, you did shut the Chief up."

"Just for that," growled Green, "you will buy me my second drink tonight."

"Will I? Who's buying the first?"

"You are. And keep your mind on your driving. I know I'm getting hungry and thirsty, but I can wait an extra few minutes to get to Colesworth."

They went straight to the Albatross Hotel. As they entered, Green said: "Pretty lush, this. But I don't like the way the carpet goes up the wall. I prefer paper myself."

"Bill Green!"

It was Crewkerne. The big, bulky D.C.S. had been waiting in the foyer to greet them. Now he ambled forward like a muscle-bound grizzly bear.

"Aubrey the Crook!" cried Green, moving to meet him.

"Old Home Week," grunted Reed. "Now the Chief's at it, too."

Masters said: "It was good of you to book us in, Mr Crewkerne, and better still of you to be here to meet us."

"Still got the old charming manners, have you, young Masters? I always thought life in the Met would knock them out of you."

"He keeps his end up," said Green. "How've you been keeping, Aubrey?"

"On top of the world till this business today. Now I'm a bit singed."

"Cheer up. His Nibs here has the case half-solved already. Have you had dinner?"

"Not yet. I was waiting for you."

"Excellent," said Masters. "If you could give us a few minutes to settle in, we could meet again in the bar."

They were all sitting round a table in the bay window of the bar, drinks in front of them. Crewkerne said: "The point is this, George. The pathologist—and he's the real forensic McCoy—says it's tricky. Technically, that is."

"The death itself?"

"Yes. Fatal thrombocytopenia, if I've pronounced it right. I'd never heard of it until this afternoon. I'd never heard of blood dyscrasias either, but evidently there's scores of 'em, all caused by different things. Professor Haywood—that's the pathologist—advised my guv'nor to get a specialist team if he could."

"And you agreed?" asked Green, surprised.

"Yes. I told him to get you lot."

"You could have done it yourself. Hell, Aubrey, you've bottomed more problems in your time than . . ."

"I know. But I wanted an outside team because of all that claptrap in the news. I want it to be seen we're not covering up. And for that reason, though I'll give you any co-operation you might need, I'm not going to offer to help or suggest that any of my people should help—barring answering your questions, of course. It's got to be a genuine third-party investigation. So after I've had a bite to eat with you here—for old times' sake—I'm going to leave you severely alone unless you approach me. I'm telling you so you won't take it amiss and think I'm sulking because you've been called in."

"We understand," said Masters. "We'll bother people as little as possible."

"Good. Let me get some more beer in."

"Not before we eat, Aubrey," said Green. "I'm oppressed with the two weak evils."

"What the hell . . . oh, you mean your bladder is . . . ?"

"Age and hunger," snorted Green. "Doesn't anybody round here know any Shakespeare?"

"His bladder's all right, sir," said Reed to Crewkerne. "It should be. He exercises it to the full often enough, if you'll pardon the expression."

"Lubricates it well every day, does he?"

"Yes, sir. And usually at other people's expense."

"I'm pleased to hear it," grinned Crewkerne. "Because though I'm not so hot on Shakespeare, I do know that little rhyme . . . how does it go, now? Ah, yes . . . 'As men draw near the common goal, Can anything be sadder Than he who, master of his soul, Is servant to his bladder?'."

"I wish you'd shut up, you lot," said Green, getting to his feet.

"Talking about it like that brings it on—like whistling in hospital."
He stalked out and the rest followed him to the dining room.

Green was first down to breakfast the next morning. He had asked
if the chef would fry him some potato to have with his bacon, egg,
tomato and sausage. His request was granted, but his order took a
little longer to prepare than just the scrambled egg that Masters
had chosen, and as Green had neglected to arm himself with a
newspaper, the others were well into their meal while he was still at
a loose end.

"Where are we going to start, George?"

Masters emptied his mouth and looked up from his *Telegraph*.
"With Snell."

"You've definitely decided on him?"

"I'm open to suggestions."

"Your usual ploy is to start with the victim and work outwards.
This time you're proposing to start on the edge of the circle and
work inwards despite the fact that last night you said you were
going to ignore the involvement of the local police."

Masters laid the newspaper aside. "True. What I meant,
however, was that I was intending to ignore the part the newsmen
have ascribed to them."

"Can Snell tell you anything you don't already know, Chief?"
asked Reed.

"I'm working on a second-hand report so far. I'm tolerably
certain it won't have contained everything we could learn from the
locals."

"True," agreed Green, rubbing his hands together appreciatively as the waiter came up with his laden plate.

"And," said Masters, "there are one or two things that seem to
have been left out. First off, I want to know where Snell got the
information that he gave to Watson concerning the relationship
between Pam and Boyce. There's somebody there who must have
felt inimical towards the lad, otherwise why grass about him to
Snell?"

"Good spud, this," said Green. "He's done it just how I like it.
Let it brown to the bottom of the frying pan so that there's a layer of

49

crispy. And he's used bacon fat to fry it in."

Reed raised his eyes in mock despair and then said: "The second point, Chief? You said there were two."

"What I said about second-hand reports not giving us the right feeling about a case. Have you got the same impression as I have about events in the nick the night before last? To me it sounds as if everything took place in a deserted building with no witnesses other than the people directly involved. I want to know who else entered the station that night and if they saw anything. After that . . ."

"There's more?" asked Green, reaching across for the toast rack.

"There's just one minor item of information that has been denied us so far—the identity of the poison. Until we have that titbit we shan't know what to look for, so we may as well use the time until then getting to know the chief protagonists."

"True," said Green. "I like it here. I reckon the chef put a few bits of finely chopped onion in this spud. Like the Germans do. Makes it very tasty."

"Go on, Chief," urged Berger. "We don't have to sit in silence and listen to him eat, do we?"

Green waved his fork menacingly at Berger, but his mouth was too full for him to reply to the sergeant's remark.

Masters smiled. "How much thinking have you done about the case, Sergeant?"

Berger reddened. "Well, Chief, when I hit the sack last night . . ."

"You fell asleep immediately? Why not? It's a good thing to do."

"But you didn't, Chief," suggested Reed.

"Actually, I did. But before then, the D.C.I. and I conferred for a few minutes. We came to no definite conclusions—hence his question as to where we would start this morning. But we did unearth what we think could be a significant fact."

"Can you tell us?"

"Did you note the time at which Snell says he approached Watson and told him of his daughter's involvement with Boyce?"

"Lunchtime, Chief. But what does it matter?"

"Lunchtime, certainly."

50

Berger and Reed glanced at each other in bewilderment. Green pushed his plate away, wiped his mouth on his napkin and drew his coffee cup towards him. "Think, lads," he said.

"What about?"

"Put yourself in Snell's shoes. If you'd heard a bit of news which concerned your sergeant as personally as that bit of gossip did, when would you tell him?"

"As soon as possible."

"Right. Go on."

Reed sat up. "I get it. The earliest possible moment the inspector could speak to Watson was when he returned to the nick after the morning court hearings."

"Now you're thinking."

"So . . . yes, that's it! Snell got his information during the morning, and as he was in the court building all the time . . . that would be odd, Chief. I don't reckon many of us get tip-offs in courtrooms."

Masters shrugged.

Reed went on: "So the grass was somebody who was there at the court and who had a grudge against Boyce. He heard of the lenient sentence given those yobs and that disappointed him, so he eased the grudge by grassing to Snell."

"The important thing is," said Green, "that we are on our way to establishing that there could be somebody with a grudge against Boyce."

"Could be?" asked Berger. "Don't you mean 'there is'?"

"No," said Masters firmly. "If we meant that, we would have to ask ourselves why Inspector Snell, knowing about the grudge, hadn't hauled this chap in for questioning."

"And the answer to that," said Green, "is nasty."

"Dereliction of duty or worse," said Masters.

"So, where does that leave us, Chief?"

"It means we are going to insist that Snell discloses the name of his informant."

"He won't like it, Chief."

"Then he'll have to lump it, won't he?" said Green. "Either he tells us, or he leaves himself open to suspicion."

"And that," said Masters, "is why I want to see Snell first. The D.C.I. and I will deal with him. You two will see Watson and Sutcliffe. After that, there are Boyce's two pals, probably Pam Watson . . . but I don't really know until the pathologist lets us know how the lad was poisoned."

Colesworth police station boasted a recreation room. It was, in fact, a basement just big enough to take a table-tennis table, a dartboard, a dozen folding chairs and very little else. It was one of three choices offered, apologetically, to Masters as his Incident Centre. The other two were Snell's office and a cupboard-like interview room.

"This will suit our purpose," said Masters to Snell. "I don't want to upset your routine work by turning you out of your office and the interview room is a little claustrophobic for four of us."

"Anything I can bring in to help you, sir, I will."

"I'm sure. Thank you. If there's anything we want, we'll ask for it, but I can't see us being here all that much. However, Mr Snell, I shall hope to keep you fully informed of the progress of the investigation."

Snell looked surprised. "That's good of you, sir, but Mr Crewkerne specifically said that he didn't want any of us locals to be involved."

"I am aware of that and I shall do my best not to involve you, but the time could come when local knowledge would be invaluable. If that happens, I shall call on you without hesitation."

"Yes, sir. Understood."

Masters turned to Reed and Berger. "Go and find Sergeant Watson and Constable Sutcliffe. Talk to them."

Reed and Berger left the recreation room. Snell glanced from one to the other of the Yard men. Masters, sensing the local man's rising apprehension, said:

"Don't worry, Inspector. We're not A10, you know."

"No, sir."

"Son," said Green, "what's your first name?"

"Roy."

Snell was impeccable in uniform, but he had a strained look in his eyes, as though the events of the last few days and the prospect of being questioned by Masters was playing havoc with his nerves. He started visibly when Green said: "Well, Roy, lad, draw up a chair. His Nibs has announced his intention of starting with you."

Snell sat down gingerly. It seemed that in spite of Masters' reassurance he anticipated being put through the hoop.

"Now, Roy," said Green, sitting beside Masters across the table from Snell, "we want to talk to you about your sources of information."

"My sources of information, sir?"

"Yes, lad. Narks, grasses . . . whatever you call them in this neck of the woods."

Snell sat silent, unwilling to be forthcoming.

"Who informed you of Pam Watson's liaison with Boyce?" asked Masters.

"Sir," began Snell, "you know it's an unwritten law that we don't disclose . . ."

Masters held up a hand to stop him.

"Don't go on. You're making a fool of yourself, Roy."

Snell reddened. "Sir, that is an uncalled-for remark."

"Just listen for a moment and then see if you change your mind."

"Sir . . ."

"Listen, lad," counselled Green.

"Regard me as a hostile investigator for a few minutes, Roy," ordered Masters. "I'm out to get you. This is my story to Mr Crewkerne concerning you."

Snell sat wooden-faced.

"Inspector Snell received information concerning Pamela Watson and Norman Boyce. This he passed on to Sergeant Watson. The thing to note is, that this information was passed to the sergeant at lunchtime on the day the three young men appeared in front of the magistrates. My belief is that the inspector, being a friend and colleague of Watson, would impart such information as this at the first possible moment. I deduce, therefore, that the inspector gathered his information during the hours immediately before lunch. But as he was in the court building

53

throughout that time, it is logical to suppose that the information was passed inside the court building.

"If this is so, I am at liberty to assume that the inspector's informant—already proven to have an interest in Boyce's movements—had heard that Boyce had been found not guilty by the magistrates. Had the informant been friendly towards Boyce, this verdict would have pleased him. The reverse could be said to be true. Why should the informant grass to the inspector unless he—the informant—was disappointed by the verdict? To grass suggests ill-will. In other words, the inspector was well aware that there was somebody who bore Boyce a grudge. On that same day, somebody with a grudge against Boyce murdered the lad. Yet Inspector Snell told nobody that he knew of a person who held a grudge against Boyce. In a member of the public, this would be a criminal offence—withholding information. In a senior police officer, it is, at the very least, dereliction of duty and, at worst, gives me grounds for suspecting that Inspector Snell is shielding the man who could have murdered Boyce. This, in my opinion, could lead to a charge against Inspector Snell equal to that of murder—namely, as an accomplice after the fact . . ."

"Stop, sir! Stop!" Snell did not sound desperate. Rather that he was angry, as though he had bottled up the interjection to a point where he could no longer keep it in.

"Stop?" asked Masters gently.

Snell exhaled. "Sir, you know this is absolute rubbish."

"Do I? As a friendly investigator I would probably agree with you. But as a hostile one . . . Look, Roy, all sorts of interpretations can be put on the most innocent of acts. As I have demonstrated, I could wheel you up in front of your superiors and make out a very good case against you if you decided to continue to shield your informant. On the other hand you could partially demolish that case were you to give us the name we are seeking."

Snell opened his mouth in surprise. "Only partially, sir?"

"Of course, lad," grunted Green. "You should have been on to that chap like a sparrow on a crumb as soon as you heard that Boyce had not died naturally. You knew he didn't like Boyce, didn't you?"

54

"No!"

"You what?"

Snell leaned forward. "You were very clever, Mr Masters, but you got it all wrong."

"I did say it was speculation," murmured Masters. "But I shall be interested to hear how I was wrong."

"The information was given to me not to ease a grudge against Boyce, but out of gratitude to the police and resentment against the magistrates. I have not withheld vital information . . ."

"Tell us, Roy," invited Green wearily, "because this I have to hear."

"Every word," instructed Masters. "Leave nothing out."

Slowly at first, and then at a more natural pace, Snell described the court hearing against Joe Howlett. How Miss Foulger had lectured him, how he had been impertinent to Mrs Hargreaves, and the conversation in the corridor. He even described the magistrates and what Howlett had told him of his immediate intentions. When he had finished he looked up at Masters and asked: "Would you call that sheltering the name of a suspect?"

"Yes, lad," said Green. "We can see how and why you regard this tramp, Joe Howlett, as a harmless old man unlikely to be connected with Boyce's murder. But you're wrong about the D.C.S. getting it wrong. He got it right. He sussed out when and where you got your whisper. He was right about the grudge . . ."

"But not about a grudge against Boyce."

"A grudge," said Green solemnly, "is a grudge. It's a feeling which affects the mind. It troubles people mentally. This old boy may have had his grudge sparked off by Miss Foulger, but like a lot of grudges, it began spilling over to splash on other people. Howlett was showing the signs, otherwise he wouldn't have shopped Boyce."

"He didn't shop him."

"He showed envy," said Masters. "Envy because those three got off. Besides meaning resentment, a grudge can mean envy. Whatever causes it, it can result in ill-will. Ill-will shown in this case by the snippet of information he gave you. You attribute it to gratitude to the police, but I could argue that gratitude is not as strong a motive as resentment."

"Couldn't have put it better myself," said Green, "so, you see, Roy, you'd be wrong to run away with the idea that His Nibs was on the wrong set of rails."

Snell shrugged helplessly. "I see I was wrong not to have gone after Howlett, but the need to name him never arose."

"Inspector," said Masters quietly. "don't become like one of those witnesses who retort that they didn't tell what they knew because nobody ever asked them. You've got to think and act—as I'm sure you do for the most part—above and beyond the normal boundaries."

"Yes, sir. I should have acted differently."

"Most surely you should. Now, I think that's over, and we could do with some coffee. Stay with us, Roy. I'd like to chat a bit more."

Snell didn't look as if the idea appealed to him very much, so Masters added, "But if you'd rather disappear . . . ?"

"There's the routine work to be done, sir."

"Mustn't keep you from that, son," said Green.

"In that case . . ."

"Just one thing, Roy," said Masters. "Have you somebody who could act as a local guide? I know I promised not to involve your people, but if you had a cadet handy, one who knew the district, it would help."

"No cadets, sir. It's only an inspector's station, you see. But I could let you have a W.P.C. She's young, but she was born and brought up here and would make a good guide."

"Is she bright?"

"They don't come any brighter, sir."

"In that case we'll accept. What's her name?"

"W.P.C. Prior, sir. Betty Prior."

"If she were to wear civilian clothes she would be less conspicuous and the link between you and us would be less obvious."

"She'll have civvies in her locker, sir."

"Good. Please send her down."

"With coffee?"

"Oh, yes please. Tell her to bring some for herself and if you

56

wouldn't mind asking her to find Reed and Berger and to bring them along, too, if they're finished, that is, I'd be grateful."

Snell left them, patently pleased to be free.

Green took out a battered packet of Kensitas and lit up. "Yon's not a frightened man exactly, but he's shaken."

"So he should be. Sticking to that damned old shibboleth about protecting sources of information! It's fine in a young copper, but when you get to his rank you've got to know when to discard tenets which are inappropriate, old-fashioned, generally abandoned or—as in this case—downright dangerous."

Green grunted, whether in agreement or the opposite was not clear. Masters got to his feet to fetch a tin ashtray from a small table near the dartboard. As he sat down, there was a bump on the outside of the door. He immediately rose again to open it. As he did so, a girl in uniform came stern first into the room, carrying a large tray.

"W.P.C. Prior, I presume?"

"Yes, sir. Sorry, sir, but I hadn't a free hand."

Masters took the tray. "Thank you Miss . . . shall we call you Betty? . . . you were very quick."

"I didn't stop to change out of uniform, sir. I thought I could do it while you had coffee."

"Right. But get back here as quickly as you can."

"Inspector Snell asked me to say your sergeants would be down almost immediately, sir."

"Thank you."

"Pretty little bit of capurtle," said Green, who liked his females slightly on the fuller side of lean. "Beats me why young lasses like her join."

"For probably much the same reasons as men do. And although we see very little of them, most people are very appreciative of their efforts and admire not only their skill, but also their undoubted courage."

"That's a point that makes me sore," said Green. "I don't reckon we should use them when there's likely to be danger. We all know they've got courage, but that doesn't mean we should test it."

Masters agreed. He had long argued that in tricky situations male members of the force could well be more concerned to protect their female colleagues than to protect themselves or even to do the job they were concerned with at the time. But he was told that in view of the Sex Discrimination Act and Equal Opportunities Commission, the force would be leaving itself open to censure were it to discriminate in the way he wished.

He was saying something of this when Reed and Berger joined them. As they drank their coffee, Masters said: "Bill, do you think it is necessary to question Pam Watson?"

"Just to make sure, you mean?"

"You saw the report by the local detective who visited her to check up yesterday?"

Green shrugged. "Nothing in it."

"Quite."

"You're not suspecting Watson, are you, Chief?" asked Reed.

"No more than anybody else."

"He's a very decent chap, and cut-up as hell about his daughter."

"That is one of the reasons why I asked the D.C.I. if we should visit her."

"I don't get it, Chief. If you discount that news story, why bother—unless you have to, that is."

"You don't get the drift, lad," said Green. "What His Nibs means is that the girlie has given her father a rough time. If he's the decent bloke you say he is, he's probably suffering in silence, and the little madam thinks that's the end of it. But if the big guns of the Yard descend upon her she could come to realise what a bloody fool she's been and how rotten she's treated her parents. It could make her think, lad."

"And haul her back from the brink, you mean?"

"Precisely. Get her to behave herself in future." Green turned to Masters. "I suggest we think about it for a bit, George. That is, of course, unless you can't think of anything else to do."

Masters grinned. "There are several things. First off, there's Joe Howlett."

Green shook his head. "Probably harmless."

"True. But apart from investigating his movements, we could question him. I got the impression that he knows most of what goes on round here. Could be that he could give us a few whispers—as well as Snell."

Green nodded.

Berger said: "Howlett? The old tramp? Was he the one who gave the inspector his information, Chief?"

"Yes. Watson didn't know that, I take it?"

"No, sir. But he gave us quite a bit about the old boy. How he came to collect his belongings after the court and how savage he was about the women magistrates."

"Savage?"

"According to Watson, Howlett said Miss Foulger should be put down."

"Did he, now? Snell says he referred to her as a miserable old bitch. It seems to me our old tramp will definitely be worth a bit of attention. We want to know exactly what he did between the time he left here and the time when Boyce was picked up." Masters turned to Green. "Bill, if I remember rightly, Snell said something about old Joe going to a fish and chip shop."

"That's right."

"Watson said that, too, Chief. Watson had given him some tea and sugar—filled one of the old tin cans he wore round his waist with tea bags and a poke of sugar. He told Watson he was going to Berry's chip shop for some scraps—that's the stuff they skim off the top of the oil."

"I know that, lad," said Green. "When I was a choker—when a penn'orth of chips really cost a penny and a fish cost either tuppence or threepence and you could actually see the difference in size—we used to get scraps put on top for nothing. Supper rooms they used to have then. Just a few tables covered in oil cloth and some forms to sit on, but you could use them if you were a customer, and there was none of this VAT lark if you ate something on the premises. Supper rooms! Usually just a bit of the shop, sometimes the back room leading off, but they used to have it painted on the windows. *Fish and Chips. Supper Room Within.* And then they used to put the prices up on the window as well—in whitewash. Skate Knobs! You never hear of skate knobs now. And little messages like 'No pies tonight. Peas.' As cryptic as that they were. Sometimes funny and misspelt. But they were your real fish and chip shops, not the Chinese chippies you get today."

Masters said: "They always smell so good as you walk past, but they never taste as good as they smell."

"No," said Green, "because they use oil. In my day they used dripping, and put up a sign to say so. In my area it was always Webster's Pure Dripping, and you got some taste with it."

Reed said: "And yet you lot are always complaining about the thirties!"

"I don't," said Masters. "I wasn't born then."

Green shrugged. "There were some good things then. Better than they've ever been since. The trouble is we've thrown out the baby with the bathwater—in the name of progress."

Before anybody could reply to this, the door opened and Betty Prior came in. "Sorry to have been so long, sir, but there was a phone call from Division."

"Don't worry, lass," said Green gallantly. "It was worth waiting for."

As indeed it was. W.P.C. Prior was—as Snell had said—a pretty little thing, with a snub nose, big eyes and nice auburn hair. Her figure was shown off well in the floral summer dress she wore. Masters noticed that it was basically green and just the right shade for a girl with her colouring.

She stood, blushing with pleasure at her greeting and at the silence which then ensued as the four big men gazed at her like small children gravely inspecting an animal at the zoo, as though not knowing quite what to make of so unaccustomed an addition to their ranks.

Masters was the first to pull himself together.

"Betty, we want to start tracing the movements two days ago of a man called Joe Howlett."

The small nose wrinkled. "The smelly old tramp, sir?"

"That's the one."

"Sergeant Watson told me he was sober, honest and a true conservationist."

60

"Meaning, I suppose," said Green, "that he doesn't drink, doesn't nick things and what else?"

"Makes good use of everything, sir. Old cans, bits of old string and so on."

"Right," said Masters, "lead on. He said his first port of call was to be Berry's fish shop."

"That's in the High Street, sir."

They trooped after the girl. Berger moved alongside her as they went. "Betty," he whispered, "the Great I Am is usually referred to as Chief, not sir."

"He might be cross if I call him that."

"Try him."

"He's very important, isn't he?"

"Very. And very good. So just play it calm and straight. Don't get windy at being with him."

"Thanks for the tip."

She led them past the desk where Sergeant Watson was working and out into the sunlight. "Right, along here, Chief." She said it hesitantly and appeared to gather courage because he seemed to accept the form of address.

"I think old Joe wouldn't go into the front shop, Chief."

"How do you mean?"

"There's a preparation shed at the back. I think that's where he'd go, because that is where he sometimes worked."

"Take us that way, please."

They followed Joe Howlett's route exactly, and came to the wide open garage doors in the back street. A massive woman was standing by the sink, cutting up fillets of white fish on a board and throwing them into a bath of water. She looked up as Masters approached her.

"Excuse me, could you tell me if Mr Berry is about?"

"Who wants to know?"

"It depends who's asking."

She turned to face Masters with the filleting knife she had been using still grasped in her great right hand. The blade had been almost honed away with years of use. It was pointed, looked razor-sharp and glistened with fish scales dotted about it like silver sequins.

61

"I'm asking."

"In that case perhaps you could tell me what right you have to ask. Mr Berry's shop assistant, perhaps?"

The growl of wrath that came from the woman's throat caused Reed, who was standing a few feet away, to move nearer to Masters either to protect him or forestall any attack with the knife.

"I'm Mrs Edna Corby. Mr Berry's my father."

"Then would you mind telling me if your father is at home?"

"No he flaming isn't. I'm looking after things here for him."

"Good."

"What's good about it?"

"You'll be able to answer my questions."

"An' just what makes you think I'm going to answer anybody's flaming questions?"

"Your commonsense, I hope. I'm a police officer . . ."

"At bloody last! It's only taken you two flaming days to get here and the nick's not a quarter of a mile away." She looked about her. "An' when you do flaming-well come, there's five of you. What's up? Too flaming frightened to come on your own to say you haven't got the bastard that did it?"

Masters let her finish.

"Mrs Corby, I haven't any idea what you're talking about."

"What I'm talking about? My flaming complaint, of course."

"What complaint was that?"

"The one I phoned the nick about on Tuesday night."

"Tuesday night?"

"Yes. Tuesday night. The night before flaming last if you haven't got enough gump to know today's Thursday."

Green grinned. He knew Masters wouldn't like that remark from this hoyden. She really was the most repulsive, domineering, asexual female he could ever recall seeing—with the exception of some of Disney's characters like the witch and Cruella. For her to get across Masters just had to be good for a laugh.

"What was the gist of your complaint?"

"Gist? Is that what you call it? I phoned the nick to tell them that some bastard had put dog muck in both my flaming wellies. I'd left them here, beside the sink, and when I came back and put them on

". . . and you say you flaming-well don't know anything about it."
She waved the knife, menacingly. "You useless great lumps of . . .
you're worse than the stuff in my wellies. Get out of here you
good-for-nothing bastards."

Masters stood his ground.

"Actually, I'm not from the local police station, so I couldn't be
expected to know about your complaint. But now I do know, I shall
see that it is looked into. In fact, Mrs Corby, I'm from Scotland
Yard, and I'm here about an entirely different matter."

"And what may that be?"

"I'm tracing the movements, on Tuesday, of a Mr Joe Howlett . . ."

"That filthy old bastard!"

"Yes. Did he call on you about lunchtime on Tuesday?"

"Yes, he flaming-well did."

"For some scraps from the pans, wasn't it?"

"That's what he came for, but he didn't get any."

"There were none?"

"There was plenty, but I wasn't giving them to that mucky old
tramp. Makes me sick just to look at him, he does. I told him to be
on his way or I'd turn the hose on him."

"And did you?"

"What?"

"Turn the hose on him?"

"Yes I flaming-well did. On his back."

"Why?"

"Because he wasn't for moving."

"No? And yet you put the hose on his back. That suggests that he
had at least turned to go, even if he hadn't actually started away."

"He was flaming cheeky, the old bastard."

"In what way?"

"He called me a fat bitch, that's what. And he said I'd have been
put in a circus if they could have found a tent big enough. So I let
him have it, right between the flaming shoulder blades. Do him no
harm, either, a bath wouldn't, the filthy old ragamuffin."

"I see. And which way did he go then?"

"To the left."

"Thank you, Mrs Corby. I'll look into your complaint, but I think I should warn you against using your hose on anybody else. It is an assault, and you could be jailed for it."

"Jailed? Get out! For giving that dirty old tramp a wetting? They'd give me a medal."

Masters turned and made his way to the pavement where Berger and Betty Prior had stayed throughout the encounter.

"I think we should go back to the station," said Masters quietly.

"You're not going on, Chief?" asked the W.P.C.

"Not for the moment. We'll call at the station and then have lunch. We shall probably be coming back this way this afternoon."

"In that case, would you excuse me for a moment?"

"Of course . . . why?"

She turned and nodded along the street. A bank of clouds of smoke had begun to roll over the back wall of a building forty or fifty yards further down the street. "I'd better see what all that's about."

"Go with her, Berger. We'll wait."

As Berger and the W.P.C. hurried along, Masters, Green and Reed strolled behind them.

"She was a bit of a ripe one, Chief. Mrs Corby, I mean. She looked like a woman blacksmith to me."

"More like one of the avenging furies," said Masters. "I wasn't too sure of that knife."

"She could have spitted you with it," agreed Green. "But I think Reed and I would have got her before she'd done more damage than that."

"Thanks."

"Not at all. It's what we aim for on these occasions—the least damage to the fewest number . . . ah, I see those two are having trouble getting in."

The gate to the back garden in which the bonfire had been lit was wedged at the bottom with a piece of wood. Betty Prior used her weight against it, but though it gave at the top, the bottom remained solid.

"Here, let me have a go." Berger was a big young man. He put his shoulder firmly against the sagging, wooden gate and, by putting his finger into the round latchpole, tried to get enough lift to clear the obstacle. He was partially successful, and opened up a gap a couple of inches wide at his first attempt. He was preparing for a further onslaught when a man's voice asked querulously: "What are you doing?"

"Open up," commanded Berger. "You're smoking out the whole neighbourhood."

"Who are you?"

"Police."

"Stop pushing, then. I had to wedge it to stop people coming in to scrounge. I had one on Tuesday at lunchtime, snooping around."

Berger stood away, the gate was forced back into its normal position and the wedge kicked out by the man inside.

When the gate was opened, a small, bespectacled man in late middle age, dressed in dirty slacks and an old shirt, confronted them. His voice when he addressed them was courteous enough. "Police, you say? What do you want?"

"It is an offence," said W.P.C. Prior, "to build any form of bonfire within thirty feet of a public highway. This one is less than six feet away from the road, and look at the size of it."

Berger was already trying to dismantle the huge heap of cartons, boxes, paper and cardboard. "What the hell have you got here, mate?"

"I have just finished trading from my shop—after over thirty years. As I hope to let the premises, I decided I had to clean them up."

"And this is the accumulated junk of thirty years?" Berger kicked a flaming carton into a clear area and stamped on it. "Get some buckets of water or a hose, man, and put it out. Then hire a refuse skip and get it carted away." He looked round the yard. "You've got enough old bottles and junk here to fill a skip." He pointed to a carboy in a wickerwork basket. "I hope things like that are empty."

"It's been empty for twenty years. I don't know why I kept it."

"To make a bottle garden, perhaps. Come on, now, friend, get that water before the whole shooting match goes up."

"Having trouble?" asked Green, appearing at the gate.

"Nothing a few buckets of water won't put right."

"I've got a better idea," said Green. "Tell your friend to nip down the road to the chippie and ask Mrs Corby if she'll lend him her hosepipe."

"You're joking, of course," grunted Berger, using a piece of wood to drag the ignited material out of the heap.

"Not at all. If the excursion doesn't result in putting his fire out, it's guaranteed to cool his ardour."

The shopkeeper returned carrying a plastic bucket of water.

"It's all yours now," said Berger. "Make sure you finish it off properly. And for heaven's sake don't wedge that gate again. If there'd been an emergency in here we'd have had a hell of a job getting in."

"Sorry about that. But you know how it is. When you've got a heap of junk like this, some people can't resist coming in to pick it over. I didn't want the rubbish strewn from here to kingdom come, so I tried to keep them out."

Betty Prior slung her bag over her shoulder, opened it and took out a packet of finger wipes. As she handed Berger a sachet, she said: "I shan't be reporting this, but make sure it doesn't happen again. It's both dangerous and unhygienic."

"That's telling him, lass," said Green as he escorted her away from the shopkeeper who stood open-mouthed watching her go.

"More water, dad," said Berger as he followed. "Get the bucket chain going." Berger smelt his fingers, then the damp tissue with which he had been cleansing them. "Good lord, I smell like the Queen of Sheba's armpit." Disgustedly he threw the little square of paper on to the rubbish pile.

Chapter 4

MASTERS MADE STRAIGHT for the desk when he reached the station.

"Are you Sergeant Watson?"

"Sir."

"How d'you do. We haven't met, but my name is Masters and this is D.C.I. Green."

"Sir," said Watson again.

"There's something I would like to see, Sergeant."

"Yes, sir."

"The Incident Book with all Tuesday night's occurrences."

Watson pushed the heavy ledger across to Masters. "It's all there, sir. Thankfully I was very careful to log all that business to the minute. I suppose you could say I had a feeling about it. At any rate you could say my head was more than full of the name Boyce that night."

"I'm sure it was. Are you going home to lunch?"

Watson shook his head. "I'm staying out of the way as much as I can, sir. Just for a bit. The wife is calming the girl down gradually, and I don't want to interfere, like."

"Stay if you wish, of course, Sergeant," said Masters. "But don't distance yourself from your daughter. I think she must be in great need of her father's friendship just now, and if you stay away, she could think you are deliberately withdrawing your love."

"I'd never do that, sir."

"I'm sure you wouldn't, but you mustn't give your daughter a chance to think you would."

"I hadn't looked at it like that, Mr Masters. Thanks for the advice. I reckon I will go home after all."

"Good. But before you go, would you mind coming down to the recreation room? W.P.C. Prior can relieve you at the desk for a few minutes."

"Now, sir?"

"Give me five minutes and then come along. It will give me time to fill my pipe and just glance at these timings."

"Right, sir."

As Masters moved away, he called: "Betty, I'd like you to come down now, with us."

Green grinned. He knew Masters wanted to keep the W.P.C. away from Watson so that she could not warn him about the Corby complaint. He wondered what excuse Masters would give the girl. He was soon to know.

"Do you know Boyce's two friends, Betty?"

"Lawson and Mobb, Chief? Yes, by sight."

"Tell me about them."

"It's the usual story, Chief. They left school a year ago and have never had a job. So they congregate and drift."

"They break into houses and vandalise them?"

"We think they've struck five times, Chief, but nobody could get the necessary evidence. That's why Inspector Snell told off P.C. Sutcliffe to keep an eye on them."

"As a sort of special project?"

"Yes, Chief. But Len Sutcliffe pounced too soon. He caught them in the act of breaking in and before they did any damage."

"I see. They damaged property. Did they ever harm people—physically, I mean?"

"Not that we know of, Chief."

"Did they ever play vicious practical jokes?"

"Like lacing that woman's gumboots with dog droppings, you mean?"

"That sort of thing."

"Not that I know of, Chief."

Masters sat back. "Thank you. Stay where you are for a moment while I look at the book, then you can take it back to the desk when you go to lunch."

He opened the ledger and found the correct page. For perhaps a minute he read it, absorbed by what was there. Then he raised his eyes to look at Green. The D.C.I., divining this as an unspoken request to step forward and see for himself, did so, and remained silent after reading over Masters' shoulder.

"Is . . . is it there, Chief, Mrs Corby's complaint?" asked W.P.C. Prior.

"Yes, Betty. Entered by Sergeant Watson at nine-seventeen on Tuesday night."

"Oh! Then he'll have told somebody to look into it."

"I don't think he did. Wouldn't you have heard if he did? Wouldn't your colleagues here have talked about being asked to investigate such an unusual and bizarre happening?"

"Perhaps he forgot because of what happened soon after that," suggested Betty.

"Probably, although . . ." Masters was interrupted by a knock on the door and the entrance of Sergeant Watson.

"Ah! There you are, Sergeant. Right, Betty, scoot. Look after the desk until the relief comes on, then have your lunch and be ready at two o'clock."

"Yes, Chief."

"Sit down, Tom," said Green when the girl had gone. "We want a quick word with you."

"About Tuesday night's timings? They're all there."

Masters said: "Not the timings, Tom. I'll let Mr Green deal with it." He made a great play of lighting the already packed pipe while Green, who understood that Masters felt that Watson would be more comfortable talking to him than to a Chief Superintendent, drew the ledger towards him.

"Tom, we've got to enquire about comings and goings in the nick on Tuesday night while you were on the desk. Just in case there were any witnesses to any part of it. People you've all forgotten about because of Boyce's death."

"Understood, sir. It was a quiet night at the desk. Until after we'd discovered Boyce was dead, that is, then it started going like a fair."

"I'm sure it did. But cast your mind back. You came on at eight, didn't you? Now, who came in from the outside world after that?"

"Well, sir . . . there was one party of three—a man, woman and child who came to ask the way to the Earlsfield Estate—that's a new lot of houses just been built on the edge of the town."

"What time?"

"About eight-thirty, I'd say, sir. Then there was a bit of a lull until a man called Gillingham came in."

"What did he want?"

"He's the father-in-law of one of our young constables. His wife wanted to leave a book for her daughter and didn't want to travel right across Colesworth with it. The young copper was to pick it up."

"Time?"

"Well after nine. I know that, because Gillingham said he'd got less than an hour's drinking time left."

"Who next?"

"I don't think there was anybody else. Oh, yes, a chap came in to show his vehicle documents after a routine road check."

"So you weren't exactly run off your feet that night?"

"No, sir. It was very quiet."

"Plenty of time to think about things?"

Watson grimaced. "I'd got plenty to think about, sir. I only wish I had been busier."

"Then why didn't you think about the phone calls you received?"

"Phone calls, sir?"

"Yes. Complaints."

Watson shrugged. "There were only two came in that night from the public. There was a bit of radio traffic but not much . . ."

"The public calls."

"What about them, sir? I know one was from one of our women magistrates. She'd had a few bottles of home-made wine knocked off a shelf in an outhouse. Probably a cat had walked along behind them and edged them off. But seeing who she was, I sent a P.C. to investigate."

"Quite right," agreed Green, consulting the book. "That was at three minutes past nine."

"Yes, sir."

"And at seventeen minutes past nine, there was another complaint."

"That's right, sir. From a woman who had found dog muck in her boots."

"What did you do about it?"

"Nothing, sir. You surely wouldn't expect me to send a constable to look into something like that, would you?"

"No. But I would have expected you personally to do something."

"Me, sir? I was on the desk . . ."

"Quite. Now think, Tom. There are three entries only in the book for that night—before midnight, that is. The last of them is the Boyce episode all neatly documented."

Watson nodded in agreement.

"The first of them is from Miss Foulger. Didn't it even strike you as a coincidence, when you were entering the Boyce details, that your book on Tuesday night should have incidents concerning not only the lad who was brought in, but also the magistrate who had heard his case that morning?"

Watson scratched his head. "Well, sir . . . I suppose you could say it was a bit funny them both being there . . . a coincidence, like you said, but I didn't pick it up. Is it important?"

"Let's see, shall we?" Green took out his crumpled Kensitas packet and offered it across the table. Watson accepted the cigarette with a word of thanks, but there was a furrow of worry on his brow as he leaned forward to do so.

"Mr Green," he said. "I don't know what you're getting at. I'm out of my depth with you."

"Oh? How come, lad?"

"I've had a word with Inspector Snell."

"Oh yes? What about?"

"About your interview with him."

"And?"

"Well, he didn't tell me what was said, but he came up from here saying you could twist any word or any action, even if it was innocent, into a hangman's rope."

"He was being critical, was he?"

"No, sir. Not critical. In fact, I thought he was admiring the way you did it, but as if he was feeling a bit sore at having been on the wrong end, like."

Masters broke in.

"Did your inspector say nothing of the subject matter of the interview? Nothing at all of what was said?"

"No, sir, he wouldn't do that. If it was confidential he'd never say a word."

Masters smiled. "I wasn't suggesting Mr Snell would be indiscreet, but what I spoke to him about concerned you in a way."

Watson looked surprised. "Oh yes, sir? Oh, of course! Boyce!"

"No, no. Mr Snell gave you some information about your daughter."

"He did that, sir."

"I wanted to know who his informant was. Do you know, by any chance?"

Watson's face set stubbornly. "I don't know who it was, sir. He wouldn't tell me and, if I may say so, I don't reckon much to you getting me down here to get to know something you couldn't get out of Mr Snell."

Masters smiled. "You've got it wrong, Tom. I wasn't going behind his back. He told me who it was, you see."

"Then why . . . ?"

"I simply wanted to know if you knew or had guessed who it was."

"How could I, sir? It could have been any one of a thousand blokes. Roy Snell has been operating in Colesworth as long as I have, sir, and I know nearly everybody. How could I guess who it was?"

"How indeed! Thank you, that's all I wanted to ask you."

"But why, sir? Why should that be important?"

"To me? To you? Or to the investigation?"

"Well . . . for any reason, sir."

"I have no wish to leave you in suspense, having roused your interest and particularly on a point which concerns you so closely. So I will just satisfy your curiosity by saying that if Boyce was murdered—and I am only here because Professor Haywood is sure

72

he was—then I must locate somebody who bore him sufficient ill-will, for whatever cause, to kill him. Now it has been demonstrated that you had no cause to love Boyce . . ."

"Sir!"

"But Professor Haywood exonerated you and Sutcliffe. If I believe his word in one respect, then I must believe it in another. So I must look for somebody other than you who wasn't too well disposed towards Boyce. Common sense, Sergeant?"

"Yes, sir. Put like that, it is."

"How do you think a man who grasses to your inspector about Boyce feels about the man he has spoken about? Would you regard him as being a good friend, or the opposite?"

Watson moved uneasily on his seat. Then he said: "I hadn't thought of it that way, sir."

"So now we've cleared the point, perhaps you and the D.C.I. will continue discussing the entries in the Incident Book."

Green shrugged and squared up to face the sergeant once again. "Now, Tom, we've mentioned a coincidence—Miss Foulger and Boyce both in court together on Tuesday morning, and both in your book again on Tuesday night."

"Yes, sir. Sorry I didn't notice that, but . . ."

"Never mind that now, Tom. What I want to talk to you about is the other entry."

"The . . . er, soiled wellingtons, sir?"

"Yes. Do you remember who made the complaint?"

"A Mrs Somebody-or-other. Corby was it?"

"Yes. Now you've explained—quite rightly in our view—that you took no action. But, Tom, did you note, when you entered the complaint in the book, who Mrs Corby is?"

"No, sir, I don't think I did . . . wait a moment, yes, I did. She said she was the daughter of Berry the fish and chip man. I haven't seen her for years and I didn't recognise her married name."

"Back to Tuesday morning again, Tom. When we came in here today, you told your story to our two sergeants here. A very full story."

"It's what they asked for."

"You told them that an old tramp called Howlett said to you on

73

Tuesday morning that when he left you, he was going straight to Berry's shop."

"That's right, sir. To pick up some scraps."

"So that was another coincidence, wasn't it?"

"No, sir."

"No? Berry's fish shop mentioned on Tuesday morning—again by somebody who had been in the magistrates' court—and then mentioned again that night in your book? What's that if it isn't coincidence?"

"Put your way it may be, sir. But for me the complaint at night would have had to mention Joe Howlett, not Mrs Corby. It didn't concern Howlett."

"How do you know it didn't? You didn't make any enquiries, did you?"

Watson looked bewildered. "I know what Mr Snell meant. You can make anything mean . . . mean anything you like."

"Can I? Have I twisted anything I've said, or anything you've said?"

"No, sir, not exactly."

"What then?"

"You're saying Howlett fouled those boots. But you wouldn't say that if you'd met Joe Howlett. You've not met him. I have."

"Have you met Mrs Corby?"

"No."

"We have. She wouldn't give him any scraps. And what is more, she deliberately turned the hose on him and drenched him."

"She did what?"

"You heard."

Watson frowned. "What the hell did she do that for? I'd given the poor old boy some tea bags and sugar in one of those open tins he carried on a bit of string round his waist. If she drenched him she'd wet that lot and ruin it."

"Well, Tom?"

"Well what, sir?"

"Don't you think that your tramp—or indeed any man—after having a hose turned on him and his brew-makings would want to get back on the person who did all that to him?"

74

Watson nodded. "I know I would, sir."

"Do you still consider it impossible for Joe Howlett to have treated Mrs Corby's wellies?"

"No, sir, I don't."

"Does that mean you think it is probable that he did?"

"Yes, I do, sir, and I'll have him brought in for it."

"And what will happen to him if you do?"

Watson looked dismayed. "Oh, lor'. I was forgetting. The bench would think he'd done it to get into jail. They'd kick him out again as like as not."

"Nice, ain't it," said Green, "to be in a position where you know that any misdemeanour you commit will only result in a let-off?"

"I suppose it is, sir."

"Do you think he thinks the same applies to murder?"

Watson half-rose from his seat. "No, sir. Not Joe Howlett. He wouldn't do it."

"You said a moment ago that he wouldn't have played that game with Mrs Corby. Now you've changed your mind."

"I know, sir, but . . ."

"Didn't Howlett mutter threats against Miss Foulger in your hearing? Yes? And Mr Snell says the same."

Watson shook his head. "I just can't believe what you're suggesting, Mr Green."

Green shut the book. "Okay Tom, but we can't just take your word for it. We'll have to follow in Howlett's footsteps, literally, to see where he went and what he did last Tuesday."

"Well, sir, I can help you a bit on that. When I was going home on the bus—to see Pam—I caught sight of Joe going into Osborne's the bakers. That's on the High Street a bit past the Albatross Hotel from here. W.P.C. Prior will know where it is."

"Thanks, Tom. That's all. Nice to know that a Yard team can solve one of your minor problems for you, isn't it? How the dog muck got in the wellies or Mrs Corby steps into the fertiliser—with both feet."

They went to a nearby pub for lunch. Reed, who was buying the first round, said to Green: "You set out to baffle that poor chap."

"Not at all."

"You made sure Betty Prior didn't warn him about the Corby woman."

"His Nibs engineered that."

"After having baffled Inspector Snell."

"To the point where Snell was fighting hard to avoid arrest, lad."

"You what? Is that true, Chief?"

"More or less," agreed Masters, carefully accepting an overfull tankard.

Reed finished handing round the drinks and followed the other three to a secluded table. As he sat down, he returned to the subject.

"Look, Chief, why frighten Mr Snell and get the D.C.I. to put Watson through the hoop?"

"Because they're sloppy," said Green lifting his beer for the first great gulp.

"And you're slurpy," retorted Reed.

"Maybe," agreed Green, exaggeratedly wiping his mouth with the back of his hand. "But at least I'm making a good job of what I'm doing—demolishing this pint, that is."

Berger joined in. "You mean these people are not doing their job properly?"

"Slapdash," said Green. "Like you two."

"Now what haven't we done?"

"Thought through why we've been a bit hard on the local talent."

"I realised there'd be a reason, because the Chief doesn't go round chopping heads off without good cause. Even you aren't too hard on people at times."

"I'll be hard on you in a minute. Like suggesting that you can buy me another drink inside the next sixty seconds."

"That's your normal self," retorted Reed. He looked up. "I ordered salad sandwiches."

"Give them time," said Masters. "I'd prefer them to be fresh cut."

"Come on, Chief," said Berger. "Why the war on the Colesworth people?"

"To concentrate their minds, Sergeant. Murder is the worst crime in the calendar. When it happens, the police concentrate on it virtually to the exclusion of all else. How much more then should they concentrate when a man who is actually in their hands dies of a murderous attack?"

"They concentrated to the point where they called us in, Chief."

"Flattering to us, no doubt, but we all know that in the majority of cases a crime such as this is solved within forty-eight hours, or it drags on for ever. But they don't think about that. They leave it to us. Yet we, who have come in cold, can start our investigation and get some way with our enquiry right here in their own nick. My contention is that whether they had invited us in or not, they should have used their heads. Snell should have realised that Howlett is a possible. Whether he actually is guilty or not is immaterial. He'd ratted on Boyce and that argues a certain degree of malevolence in the old man that both Snell and Watson refused to recognise. That I am right about that is probably supported by the dirty trick he played on Mrs Corby."

"Warranted, Chief."

"That is beside the point. He could bring himself to do it. If he could introduce dog-droppings into a woman's gumboots, why wouldn't he introduce a noxious substance into Boyce's drink?"

"You're saying Howlett is the murderer, Chief?"

"Not at all. I'm saying he should have been considered and followed up yesterday by Snell. By the same token, Watson should have noted the coincidences in the Incident Book and so should Snell. That would have prompted them even further to look at Howlett. But they did nothing. And not only that, when we arrived Snell didn't want to divulge the tramp's name and Watson didn't bother himself to get round to the fish shop to see whether it was possible to establish whether Howlett could be involved."

"So now you know," said Green, "one of you lads can refill my glass."

Reed and Berger paid him no attention. They sat quiet for a moment or two before Berger asked: "And you think your tactics paid off, Chief?"

"Assuredly. We got to know Howlett's name, and where he was going. We've surmised he got his own back on Mrs Corby. Now Watson has told us he saw the tramp going into a baker's shop. We're going there after lunch. But do you think we would have got that snippet unless we'd managed to concentrate Watson's mind?"

"I suppose not, Chief."

"And in addition," said Green, "we've probably given them an idea or two which will make for better policing in Colesworth."

"Are you saying the force here is bad?"

"What do you think? Three yobs on the loose, breaking into four or five houses in a month. Snell and his merry men know this, but they say they couldn't get proof. Would you be satisfied with that, young Berger? How many jobs like that would three kids have to pull before you nailed them—given you knew their identity?"

Berger shrugged. "Not four or five, I hope. And when I did get them, I wouldn't have let them get away with it."

"Ker-rect, lad. So what is your opinion of the local bobbies?"

"Nice chaps but could do better, I suppose."

"And all they have to do to do better, lad, is to use their heads. That's what His Nibs was saying, in essence."

The sandwiches arrived. Large portions of French bread split lengthwise and overstuffed with tomatoes and other salad stuffs. The effort required to eat what Green described as "doorsteps" effectively precluded much more conversation. By two o'clock they were back at the station to find Betty Prior waiting for them.

"Osborne's the bakers, please, Betty."

"Right Chief. It's the same way as Berry's, but we stay in the High Street."

"Is it far to walk?" asked Green.

"Six or seven hundred yards, sir."

"We'll walk."

Much as visitors to an unfamiliar town will, they walked along gazing at the shops on both sides of the road.

"Where would Howlett have come back on to the High Street, Betty? After he left Berry's he continued along the back road, according to Mrs Corby."

"It runs parallel to this, Chief. His first chance of getting back to the High Street would be down the narrow road which runs just this side of the Albatross Hotel. Then he'd not have far to go to reach Osborne's."

It was a good-looking shop: double fronted with bow windows, small paned. Masters imagined that the proprietors would not be too pleased at receiving the patronage of tramps. As yet it was a little early in the afternoon for the full flow of business to have resumed, but judging by the two or three customers he saw, the shop normally catered for a section of the community unlikely to be well-disposed towards smelly old tramps.

He and Green went in with Betty.

"Can I see the manager or manageress, please?" asked Masters when the girl behind the counter offered her services. "Make sure to tell whoever it is that I'm not here to make a complaint. I'm a police officer and I'm seeking information."

The girl looked at him for a moment and obviously liked what she saw or approved of his approach. At any rate she smiled at him. "I'm sorry, but the manageress won't be back for at least half an hour. Can I help you?"

"Perhaps you can. On Tuesday—at lunchtime—an elderly tramp came into the shop."

"Oh, yes. He was wet through. Mavis served him."

"Mavis?"

The girl nodded in the direction of the opposite counter where a girl was down on her knees stacking pies and sausage rolls in a display case.

"Thank you."

"Mavis!" called the first assistant. "The police have come for you."

"For me? Damn!" Mavis, in standing up too quickly in her inquisitive enthusiasm had obviously put an unbearable strain on her tights, and one leg had laddered sadly. "That's the second pair this week. I'm just going to have to stop wearing them." She

79

straightened the skirt of the pink overall. "Police, did you say? Why? What's the matter?"

"Nothing, love," said Green. "But don't go about saying you're just going to have to stop wearing them, or people will get the wrong idea."

Mavis chuckled. Masters said: "On Tuesday—at lunchtime—a tramp came into the shop."

"Oh, yes. Old Joe Howlett."

"You know him?"

"He's been around ever since I can remember."

"Does he come in here regularly?"

"Well . . . sometimes. About once a month, I'd say. He always wants the same thing."

"What's that?"

"A yesterday's loaf. Most people like fresh bread you know. But some—like those who suffer from indigestion—like it a bit older. If we have any over, we sell it next day a bit cheaper. Five pee off, usually. That's what Joe has."

"Always the same, you say?"

"Oh, yes. We know he's been to the Albatross when he comes in here. He goes to the back kitchen door at the hotel, you know, and if they give him his cheese rind . . ."

"Cheese rind?" echoed Green.

"Yes. Stilton. You know. After it's been scooped out there's often a lot left round the inside. If they've got one like that, they give it to Joe. Then he comes in here for the bread to eat with it. I've heard him say he's often scraped enough cheese off a big Stilton case to last him a week."

"Doesn't do too bad for a tramp, does he, love? I wouldn't mind joining him if the weather's nice."

"Choose a day when I've got a couple of old sticky buns to put in with his loaf," whispered Mavis conspiratorially. "Then you could have yourself a ball."

"It's an idea," agreed Green.

"Tell me," said Masters, breaking up the tête-à-tête, "what does your manageress think of Joe Howlett coming in here?"

"He chooses his time—when we're not full up."

"How very wise of him. Just one more thing. You say you are sure he wanted bread to go with his cheese from the Albatross. Did you notice whether he had the cheese with him?"

"Now you come to mention it, I didn't see it. He usually carries it wrapped in a paper napkin . . . no, he didn't have it with him. Definitely. That's funny. Is that what you wanted to know about him?"

Masters smiled and shook his head.

"What do you want him for then? Oh, I know! He's been up to his tricks again. Doing his welly dance in the High Street."

"Something of the sort."

"What's cheese got to do with that?"

"He bunged up the exhaust pipe on the Mayor's car with it," lied Green unblushingly.

"So it wouldn't start, you mean?"

"Oh, it started all right—after a bit. But the Town Clerk got a face full of green cheese, because he was standing behind it when it fired."

Mavis covered her mouth with her hand in a vain effort to stop the laughter.

"Where to now, Chief?"

"The Albatross, Betty."

W.P.C. Prior, having been present at the conversation in the baker's shop and therefore aware that the hotel had been mentioned, showed no surprise. But Berger, to whom this was merely a pointless retracing of steps, asked: "What's this, Chief? Early afternoon tea in the lounge?"

Masters was saved from the necessity of replying by the muted sound of Betty's radio, which she was carrying in the sling bag over her shoulder. Green, however, had already made a mumbling remark about a three piece band playing *Merrie England* to help the cucumber sandwiches down when the W.P.C. said: "Message from Mr Snell, Chief. Professor Haywood will be at the station at four o'clock and would be pleased to see you there at that time if convenient to you."

Masters looked at his watch. It was barely three o'clock.

"Please ask Mr Snell to let Professor Haywood know that I shall be with him at four o'clock."

While the W.P.C. radioed the message, Green said: "We've plenty of time to call at the Albatross, George, but if you'd like me to do it while you go on . . ."

"No, Bill, thank you. I want you to be with me when I speak to Haywood."

"Right."

When they entered the hotel they were lucky enough to see the afternoon under-manager crossing the foyer in the day-time uniform of black jacket and pinstripe trousers.

"Could I have a word with you, please?"

"Certainly, Mr Masters."

Green said: "We're known, George."

The under-manager kept a straight face and added: "And your particular likes, Mr Green. For instance, I hear that you like to eat hearty at breakfast time."

"You mean I'm known more for my appetite than my professional reputation?"

"We do tend to concern ourselves here more with appetites than police investigations, sir. That's our job."

"Then you've got a shock coming, laddie. You're about to be involved in a police investigation."

"I am? The hotel is?"

"In a small way," said Masters.

"Is there something wrong, sir?"

"No. A small problem. There is a tramp in Colesworth called Joe Howlett. Do you know him?"

"I've heard of him, Mr Masters, but I can't say I've ever met him."

"Not your type at all," said Green. "Hasn't your style in dress."

The under-manager grinned. He was very young. "You should see how I dress when I'm not on duty, Mr Green. My mother disowns me in the street."

"Dirty jeans?"

"With holes and patches."

Masters said: "This man, Howlett, is in the habit, I believe, of

82

calling at your back kitchen door every now and again."

"In search of food?"

"He has a great liking, I understand, for Stilton. One of your staff sometimes saves him a case with some edible cheese still there—or so I am led to believe."

"That could well be so. If they are of no further use in the restaurant, somebody should get the benefit of them rather than us putting them in the swill bins."

"Quite. Could I see the person who would have given Howlett the cheese?"

"That may not be easy."

"Why not?"

"Because kitchen staff have a break between lunches and preparing dinners—except for our confectionery cook who bakes scones and small cakes for afternoon teas each day."

"Could we see if whoever it is is on the premises?"

"Of course, but I'm just wondering . . . you see, Mr Masters, we are a good hotel, but we're nothing like as big as some of your London ones. We don't have different chefs for every different type of dish. We don't have a man exclusively for sauces, for instance, or even for fish alone. Cheese—all sorts—is looked after by our cold-table chef and he, poor soul, has to be able to prepare everything from salmon mousse to Russian Salad, with appropriate dressings."

"Could we try him?"

"Why not? Would you like to come to the kitchen?"

Masters and Green followed the under-manager. Neither had ever entered a hotel kitchen before this moment. They were, to say the least, surprised. The great room was practically deserted. The long central bank of ovens and hot plates was cold and dead, the high servery counter empty. All the vessels seemed grey and battered—huge rectangular dripping tins and roasting dishes, fish kettles, dixies—all in grey metal. No food visible. Everything in store cupboards and cold rooms. All the utensils huge in comparison with their domestic equivalents.

And practically deserted, except for the confectionery cook who was working in a small offshoot from the main kitchen. She had several cooling racks full of individual cakes, and was whipping a large bowl of batter.

"Lucy, these gentlemen would like a word with Derek. You don't happen to know where he is, do you?"

Without a word, the woman nodded towards a door on her right. The under-manager murmured his thanks and led the way into the room. It was the kitchen staff's dining room. On the long central table a man was lying flat on his back. He wore soiled white trousers and a white zephyr, and in one outstretched hand he was holding an opened can of beer. His occupation seemed to be nothing more than gazing at a not-particularly-exciting ceiling.

"Derek."

The man raised his head and then, when he saw strangers, sat up and swung his legs to the floor.

"Scotland Yard," announced the under-manager. "They'd like a word."

"Sorry to disturb your kip, mate," said Green.

"I was about to get weaving," said Derek. "I'm cold-table, you see, and lots of my things have to be prepared early."

"To get cold?"

"That's right. And I was on breakfasts this morning so I was on the job by six."

"Are you the chap who fried that spud for me?"

"If you're the one who asked for it, I am." Derek took a swig at his can and put it down beside him on the table. "What can I do for you gents?"

"Are you the one who gave Joe Howlett, the tramp, a Stilton rind on Tuesday?" asked Masters.

"What if I am? There's no law against it, and the management doesn't mind as long as we're not fiddling stuff that can be used."

"I'm not suggesting you have done anything wrong."

"Why the questions then?"

"I was a bit surprised that Howlett should have called here at lunchtime. I thought he would have known better than to bother you at so busy a time."

"Who told you he came here at lunchtime?"

"Nobody. I guessed he did."

84

"Don't give me that—guessed!"

"It was quite easy, really. You see it is his habit to buy a loaf of bread only when you very kindly give him cheese to eat with it. He bought a loaf on Tuesday at lunchtime. To me, that didn't seem right. So I asked the shop assistant in the baker's if Howlett was carrying a package which could have been a Stilton rind. She said he wasn't. So I suspected that he had bought the loaf because he had been promised his cheese later."

"Very clever," said Derek reaching for his beer can.

"Oh, there's more," said Masters. "The cheese rind could only be ready for him after lunch or after dinner. So Howlett could have returned here early in the afternoon to collect what you had promised him. But from my own experience in hotels, I would judge that not much Stilton would be consumed at lunchtime, whereas I have seen a great deal eaten at dinnertime. So, the alternative is that you told him to return in the evening—say after the first rush of early dinners was over and a Stilton was more likely to have been finished in the dining room. Am I right?"

"Why should I tell you whether you're right or wrong? I don't know what you've got against old Joe Howlett, but the fact that you come here to ask questions about his movements shows you're after him for something. And that's a load of cods. Old Joe doesn't nick things and he doesn't hurt people, so I'm not answering your questions. If you're so good at guessing, you guess the answers for yourself."

Masters turned to the under-manager. "I think it would be wise if you were to start making enquiries about a replacement chef for cold-table duties this evening, with a possibility of tomorrow, too."

"I . . . I'm afraid I don't understand."

"Let's put it another way," said Green harshly. "We're taking this joker in. Now. He'll spend the night in the cells and appear in court tomorrow morning charged with obstructing police officers while carrying out their lawful duty, namely conducting a murder enquiry."

"Surely not?"

"If it's his first offence he could be let off or even be given a suspended sentence. But I wouldn't count on it if I was in his shoes, because if he goes into court and Detective Chief Superintendent George Masters of the Yard goes into the box against him—and you, too, of course, because you've witnessed his refusal to answer our questions—it'll be a brave set of magistrates that will let him off."

The young under-manager gazed from Green to Masters and then to Derek who still sat on the table, his mouth open in bewilderment at the turn events had taken.

"I'd have to appear in court?"

"Will have to," corrected Green. He turned to Derek. "Come on, sonny boy. There are three more like us waiting upstairs to escort you to the nick."

"You can't. You can't take me in just for not saying he came back at nine at night."

"That's when he picked up the Stilton?"

"Yeah."

"It's just as well you spoke," said Masters, "because the D.C.I. and I have an important meeting at four o'clock and we'd no more time to spare with you. It literally was a case of telling us what we wanted to know or of going inside. So don't run away with the idea we were fooling you. We never fool about on business. And don't forget if you're on breakfast duty tomorrow morning, Mr Green likes his mashed potato fried—with finely chopped onion—until it just browns on the bottom of the pan, because he likes the crispy bits."

"And make sure you cook it in bacon fat," added Green.

As they were returning through the kitchen Lucy, the confectioner, said to Green: "Well, did you get what you came for?"

"Not yet."

"Not yet? Meaning you hope to? What are you after?"

"One of those lemon curd tarts. My old mother used to make her own lemon curd in one of those old stone jam jars. But she always made her curd tarts oval."

"Oval?"

"Yes. They were bigger than the round ones. Oval tarts cost tuppence in the shops, round ones a penny."

86

"Thanks," said Lucy.

"What for, love?"

"There's a heap of those old oval patty-tins in a cupboard through there. I wondered what they were used for."

"Now you know. Lemon curds, oh! and Maids of Honour. Do you ever make those?"

Lucy grimaced. "You'd like some of those, too?"

"You mean you've made some?"

"Yes. Here you are." She slid the confectionery into a bag from a pile which the hotel obviously kept for packing lunches.

"Look what I've been given," said Green proudly to Masters, showing him the bag.

"You haven't been given them," said Lucy. "They'll be put on your bill."

"Thanks."

"With fifteen per cent VAT and ten per cent service charge."

"Thanks again."

"Not at all," she said, dredging sugar on to a row of Swiss Rolls. "If I gave them to you you could accuse me of trying to bribe the police, and if you accepted them you'd be guilty of corruption."

"Quite right," said Masters gravely. "But may I ask a question?"

"It's a free country."

"Please tell me why you are so anti-police."

"Three weeks ago yesterday," she replied, "I had my home vandalised. My husband and I have worked hard all our married lives to get ourselves a nice home. Nothing grand, of course, just a semi with nice carpets and curtains and a telly and a nice white bedroom suite . . . but you'll know. Your lot made a note of it at the time. And since then . . . not a dicky bird. Not a sign from you lot. You haven't got the ones who rubbed crap on my sitting room wallpaper and broke most of my bits and pieces. You and the insurance people! You do nothing and they kindly tell us we were under-insured, but even if we'd been fully insured we wouldn't have got full money. Oh no, you only get a proportion of the original value even though it costs twice as much to replace as it did when you bought it eighteen months ago. That's why I'm anti-police, and anti-insurance, and why those perishing tarts are going on your mate's bill!"

"I'm sorry . . ."

"Sorry? Is that all you can say? Or do you want to save your energy for killing young lads in your police stations or for hauling Derek off into court?"

Masters laughed aloud.

"I do believe you listened outside the door of the staff dining room, Lucy."

She reddened. "What if I did?"

"Nothing, except that you're already aware that I'm in a hurry and so you will excuse my having to rush away. But it has been nice talking to you."

As they walked back along the High Street, Green gave Reed, Berger and W.P.C. Prior a fairly full and accurate account of what had been said in the hotel kitchen.

"Never mind," said Berger, "we can eat your tarts with a cup of tea when we get back to the nick."

"Is that your only thought on the matter?" asked Masters. "No dismay that in this pleasant town there should be citizens who are as incensed as Lucy against the police?"

"There can't be many, Chief," protested Betty Prior.

"No? Five homes vandalised. That's five families with their outraged friends and relatives—probably a hundred people all told from those five incidents alone. And what about others, who have had their cars stolen, garden gnomes pinched—or any one of a thousand incidents which haven't been satisfactorily concluded? I don't think there's room for complacency, Betty, even in Coles-worth."

"No, Chief. But . . ."

"But what, Betty?"

"But that's not what you're here for."

"True."

"So how far did you get in your investigation by just going to the hotel and learning that Joe Howlett was given his cheese rind after dinner at night? You see, Chief, it seems to me that even some of your questions get you no further forward."

"Lass," counselled Green, quietly, "you're getting into dangerous waters."

"No I'm not. I was pointing out to the Chief . . ."

"I heard, love. But think! Howlett was at the back door of the hotel at nine that night."

"So?"

"So he was within a couple of hundred yards of Berry's shop just seventeen minutes before Mrs Corby discovered her boots had been doctored."

Betty's face showed surprise. "Of course! I never thought of that. Chief, I apologise . . ."

"More important," interrupted Green, "it means we also know that Joe Howlett was in and around Colesworth at the time young Boyce could have been poisoned . . ."

Betty's eyes opened wide.

"I have made a fool of myself, haven't I?"

"Just a bit of a one."

"It . . . it's different. The way the Chief works, I mean."

"If you mean it gets results," said Reed, "you're right, sweetheart."

Chapter 5

It was ten minutes to four when Masters and his colleagues entered the recreation room, but Haywood was there before them. He was amusing himself at the dartboard, playing a game of round-the-clock against himself. He threw the last of the current clutch of three darts as they entered, cursed himself for having missed double sixteen and turned to greet them.

"I'm Haywood. Forensic etcetera."

"Masters." The two shook hands. They were of an age, though Masters towered above the very-average sized professor. But they were a match for each other in smartness of dress and turnout: Masters in Windsor grey check with highly polished brown shoes, Haywood in light grey Palm Beach suiting with highly polished brown shoes.

"I would like to present my colleagues. D.C.I. Green, D.S. Reed, D.S. Berger and our temporary local guide, W.P.C. Prior."

Haywood waved a hand and smiled. "All the leading lights together, in fact."

"You don't mind an audience, Professor?"

"Not a bit of it. My file's over here." He moved to the table-tennis table. "But I don't think I'll need it."

"Shall we sit?"

"Would you like me to take shorthand notes, Chief?" asked Betty Prior.

"Before I say yes or no to that . . . Professor, are we going to use words that will be intelligible to a non-medical shorthand taker?"

"Depends on how closely you question me."

"He'll give you the works, Prof," grunted Green. "Give him a chance to get in among the unmentionables and unpronounceables of medicine and he'll be here till doomsday." He turned to Betty. "I tell you what, love, you go and get half a dozen cups of tea and a couple more cakes and we'll eat those I brought. Don't worry, we won't start without you, so you can take that pout off your pretty little physog."

Betty grinned and got to her feet. Masters said: "But please hurry, Betty. The Professor is a busy man."

"Meaning you're not a busy man?" asked Haywood with a grim smile after Betty had slipped out.

"The Chief's busy enough," said Reed. "He just gives the impression he isn't."

"Better that than those who try to give a false impression t'other way," said Haywood. "Now, having demonstrated that I don't fall into that category myself—by being here well before the agreed time, I think I should tell you that this little job has taken me so long because I didn't use my loaf. By that I mean I tested for a lot of common toxic agents—and failed to find them—before I had the necessary gumption to accept that an uncommon agent could have been used. I tell you that, gentlemen, just in case you've been cursing me for having kept you waiting so long for the answer."

"I knew it," said Green. "Just our luck. Why is it we never get a job where a nice, easy household substance has been used? As soon as I heard that word thrombocytopenia I guessed we were in for a dog's dinner of a case. And now the prof's just confirmed it. It makes you wonder, doesn't it?"

Haywood said: "Mr Green, would you be surprised to learn that what killed Boyce can be found in practically every household in the country? That if you went out into the High Street at this moment you would find quite a large percentage of people were carrying it about on their persons—particularly the women—and that W.P.C. Prior definitely is at this moment?"

"Definitely is what?"

"In possession of the substance that killed Boyce."

Green was saved from the necessity of making an immediate reply by the bump at the door which heralded Betty's arrival with the tray. Berger opened the door and the W.P.C. backed in, both hands fully occupied with her burden.

"Put it down here, love," said Green, regarding her closely, "and tell me what you've got on you that's poisonous."

"Poisonous? Nothing."

"The Prof says you have."

Betty looked at Haywood. "Did you say that, sir? Or are you pulling his leg?"

"It's true enough."

"What, my powder or eye-shadow or something?"

"None of those things. It's round your wrist."

She looked with surprise at the tiny watch she was wearing. "I don't understand."

"Right," said Masters. "Shall we all sit down? Betty, we have merely been gassing to fill in the time until you got back because we promised not to start without you. Take your tea, everybody. And, please, Professor, could we now begin in earnest?"

"Sure thing. But I wasn't fooling, you know."

"Maybe not, but you have me baffled, nevertheless."

"What do you think the toxic substance was that killed Boyce?"

"Please tell us."

"Gold."

There was a moment of silence.

"Gold?" murmured Masters. "I now see what you meant when you said you had found an uncommon agent."

"You say gold is poisonous, sir?" asked Berger. "In its normal state? Like Betty's watch or . . ."

"Or gold earrings or wedding rings? Yes, Sergeant. I can quote you chapter and verse, because I took the trouble to look it up. There are cases of women developing persistent, papular, eczematous lesions on both earlobes following ear-piercing and the subsequent wearing of gold earrings. Many women cannot wear gold wedding rings without getting dermatitis so seriously that they have to take them off permanently and there are cases where jewellers have developed necrotising vasculitis through their work. All these nasties have come about through simple external contact with the metal—among people who are sensitive to gold, that is. Fortunately most of us are unaffected by our jewellery. But think of the effect of gold on sensitive people if internal contact is made."

"Wait a moment, Prof!" said Green. "Are you saying that young Boyce could have swallowed a lump of solid gold, out of a tooth or something?"

"Nothing like that. I am saying he took or was given a massive dose of sodium aurothiomalate, which is a disodium salt—to give it its chemical name—but which has a gold content of roughly forty-five per cent."

"A medicine?" asked Masters.

Haywood nodded. "You must all have heard of gold injections for rheumatoid arthritis."

"I have," admitted Masters. "However, I know very little about it except that I have the impression that gold has to be administered with great caution."

"You're absolutely right. I'm no rheumatologist, but my textbooks tell me that toxic reactions are liable to occur in up to fifty per cent of patients undergoing gold therapy. In about five per cent, these reactions may be severe and, occasionally, even fatal."

"Excuse me, sir," said Reed, "but surely no medical man would use a medicine that had so much danger attached to it?"

"There is no clear cut answer to that, Sergeant, except to say, as a generalisation, that it is used as a last resort treatment when everything else has failed. Then, when it is used, the doctor will start with very small injections at very long intervals and monitor the progress and reaction of the patient. Many of them do very well on it and gain tremendous relief, but those who react badly are taken off it immediately."

"But, sir, you said that up to half of them showed toxic reactions."

"True enough, but some of those reactions are preferable—in the patient's view—to the everlasting pain of rheumatoid arthritis. What I mean is, Sergeant, that . . ."

"I think I know, sir. If I had a non-stop headache and I knew aspirin would cure it even though it gave me a pimple on my big toe, I'd choose to have the pimple rather than the headache."

"Excellently put."

"But we're not talking about pimples, are we?" asked Masters.

"I imagine the alternatives with gold therapy could be pretty horrific."

"Nightmarish."

"Scare us," said Green. "We can take it."

"Very well. How's this? Stomatitis, pruritus, erythema, papular eruptions, urticaria, exfoliative dermatitis, colitis, nephrosis, aplastic anaemia, agranulocytosis, leucopenia, thrombocytopenia and toxic hepatitis—among others. Occasionally—according to the book—there are things like haematuria, encephalitis and a few more like that. Finally, fatal blood dyscrasias may occur suddenly."

"Like in Boyce's case."

"Right. He had a massive blood dyscrasia."

"What is the average, normal dose of aurothiomalate?" asked Masters.

"It depends a bit on individual patients, but as a yardstick I would suggest an initial dose of fifty milligrams—to start them off. The next week, twenty-five milligrams, and then every week after that only ten milligrams until there was remission of pain, or evidence of toxicity."

"An ever-decreasing dose, virtually?"

"Sort of."

Masters paused a second to collect his thoughts. "That suggests there is a build-up in the body."

"Most definitely there is. It can still be traced a couple of years after cessation of treatment. And I'd like you to know that some rheumatologists go the other way about treatment. They start low and build up the amounts. Then when they have reached the top dose, they lengthen the intervals between treatments so that, in essence, the patients get the same amounts by both methods."

"Fine. I understand that. Am I right, therefore, in assuming that total amounts taken—even over a long period—are critical?"

"You certainly are."

"What are those total amounts?"

Haywood took a bite at the lemon curd tart he held in his hand before replying. As he munched, he gesticulated after the fashion of

94

a man who wants to indicate that he has something pertinent to say as soon as his mouth is empty.

"Ah!" he said at last. "There is no cut and dried answer. Each patient reacts differently. But I think you should assume—again as a yardstick—that blood dyscrasias might occur when the total dose reaches three hundred to five hundred milligrams. That is why it is stressed that patients should have a full blood count before each injection and even if the patient shows no signs of reaction, the dose should never exceed fifty milligrams. But—and this will make you realise that I can't be specific—there is, on record, a paper which says that ten patients developed dyscrasias without warning on a total dose of only two hundred milligrams."

"Fatal dyscrasias?"

"No, they were caught in time and treated, but the same paper records fifteen fatalities during gold therapy with an average dose of about seven hundred milligrams."

"This stuff is deadly," said Green sternly. "Surely the Committee on Safety of Medicines is doing something about it?"

Haywood shrugged. "They are doing what they can. And I think you will find that not so much gold is now used and certainly not used without very strict precautions."

"I should hope not."

"The next pertinent point," said Masters, "is the amount Boyce took. Presumably he must have ingested a vast amount?"

"You know how we estimate the amount ingested, don't you?"

"You measure as accurately as possible in one or two organs and then multiply by some formula or other to arrive at the total."

"Roughly right. And though it sounds a bit haphazard it is, in fact, extremely accurate. I say this because you are going to be more than a little astounded to hear that my calculation suggests Boyce's body contained upwards of two thousand milligrams."

"Two thousand! But that's . . . that would have killed anybody, I suspect, judging by what you've already told us."

"Certainly it would if it were not spread over several years. And this wasn't. Boyce took that little lot only a matter of hours before his death. That was easy to establish."

"In other words he took it all at once."

95

"That would be my guess."

Masters took out his pipe and started to pack it. Berger said: "Two thousand milligrams is what? Two grams?"

"Right. You can judge the amount better, I think, if you remember that there are roughly thirty grams to the ounce. So he took a fifteenth of an ounce."

"Not much if you say it quickly," said Green.

Masters completed the lighting of his pipe. When he had an even burn, he sat back from the table and crossed one leg over the other.

"Professor," he said, "you've given us the poison . . ."

"Sorry, Chief Super, may I interrupt for a second? I should have mentioned that Boyce had, in fact, an incipient gastric ulcer. I mention it only because it could conceivably have made absorption of the aurothiomalate that much better and quicker. I suspect that over the last year or two the young man had over-indulged in liquor."

"Thank you, Professor."

"That's all."

"Right. Now there are lots of things we've still got to ask you. First, where could he have got the gold?"

"From a doctor, a pharmacist or a person suffering from rheumatoid arthritis who had the ampoules as a supply for his or her course of injections."

Green grunted. Masters wasn't sure whether or not this suggested an idea had leapt into his assistant's mind, but he realised that almost since the professor had first started talking about gold injections he, himself, had held Miss Foulger in mind. Snell had described her as rheumaticky with misshapen fingers. Furthermore, at some unspecified time on Tuesday, there had been an intruder at her home. Had that intruder taken a supply of gold injections from the house, as well as breaking a few bottles of wine to cover up the theft? If so, it argued a knowledgeable man—or woman. One familiar with the properties of gold. And if—as seemed likely from the report in the Incident Book—Miss Foulger claimed that only her outhouse had been entered, then that fact alone would bring the magistrate even more into the reckoning. She could be the one who—because she had been treated with it—knew the properties of gold; she could be the one who had a supply; and she could be the one who had staged an apparent break-in of her own property in order to do what? Cover up the disappearance of her supply of gold?

Masters got no further with this line, because Haywood was continuing.

"I've checked up on how sodium aurothiomalate injection is supplied. There are an incredible number of strengths. One, five, ten, twenty and fifty milligram ampoules. But don't be led astray by that. They are all the same size, because they are all dissolved in the same tiny amount of water, namely one millilitre. And you can judge how much that is when you recall that the average plastic medicine spoon that chemists supply will hold five millilitres."

"The fluid will be in tiny ampoules, I take it?"

"Yes. They are packed in tens and the whole pack would be no bigger than a cigarette packet. Remember, too, that gold is light-sensitive, so the ampoules are made of brown glass—actinic glass, it is called—so that sunlight won't cause chemical change to the contents. The ampoules themselves are of the usual sort—the snap variety with a coloured ceramic snap band round the neck."

Masters waited a moment or two, and then asked: "Has aurothiomalate no taste? Wouldn't the lad have known he was taking something strange?"

"I've never tasted it myself, but the powder—from which the solution is made—is said to have a slight odour. What of, I don't know. But I think that when tiny amounts are dissolved in water there would be no more smell than there is, say, to sugar in water. You will remember, no doubt, that sugar also has a slight odour?"

Masters nodded. "And colour?"

"A fine, pale yellow. The sort of shade that would never be noticed in any other drink."

"Drink? You said that as though you thought he had taken it in some sort of booze."

Haywood shrugged. "There was alcoholic liquor in the body. I was told he had taken a couple of halves of beer, but there was more than that. He'd also taken white wine. A good amount of it. Plonk,

I suspect, but these things, liquors, tend to mingle in the body and take a bit of sorting out."

"As much as a bottle of plonk, would you say?" asked Green.

"That would be my estimate. A full bottle."

"So a bottle of wine and two beers . . . that would carry him well on the way to being blotto—which is what the constable said he was."

"Quite right. His degree of drunkenness, allied to his bodily malfunctions due to the effects of the gold, would make him appear to be absolutely plastered."

Masters said nothing. Wine! Here it was again. Miss Foulger had lost wine—or so she claimed. Could she have doctored a bottle, given it to Boyce—under the guise of a generous gesture to support her leniency in court—and then smashed the rest of the brew to disguise the fact that one bottle had gone?

Haywood drew his file towards him. "I've no need to remind you gentlemen that when a medico-legal autopsy is ordered, one of the measures that has to be taken is an examination of the clothing. This I have done.

"The young man was dressed in a T-shirt and jeans—apart from socks, boots and underpants, I mean. His clothes were surprisingly clean. I imagine he had put on clean clobber for his court appearance that morning and later removed whatever sort of jacket he had worn then. Because it has been very hot."

Masters nodded his ready agreement of Haywood's supposition and waited for the professor to continue.

"Now, although his shirt was basically clean, it was stained. I examined not only the substance that had caused these stains, but also the shape of the marks. Now I can't be absolutely certain about this, but the shapes suggested to me that Boyce had been drinking direct from a bottle or one of these ring-pull cans the young seem to accept as suitable vessels from which to take refreshment."

"You mean he had carelessly thrown his head back with the bottle or tin at his lips and some of the liquid had dribbled down his chin and on to his shirt?"

"That's it."

98

"What had he drunk?"

"Wine. And not red wine, either. The stains were very pale."

"Are you going to tell us that you found traces of aurothiomalate in those stains?"

"How did you guess?"

"So the gold was in the wine?"

"I think you can bank on that as one solid piece of fact. I know you must already have deduced that, but now you have forensic support for your deduction."

"Thank you. Anything else?"

"Should there be?"

"Did you examine his boots?"

"Yes. By that I mean I gave them the once over. I paid less attention to them than I did the shirt, because I saw nothing to warrant closer inspection."

"Thank you."

"No, don't thank me, Mr Masters. You had a reason for asking that question—no, don't tell me what it was, otherwise you will influence the second examination I am going to give them as soon as I leave here."

"I was not suggesting you have not done a thorough job, Professor. I—and all my colleagues—are more than happy with what you've done for us."

"So far, you mean."

"Steady, Prof," said Green. "His Nibs here gets strange ideas at times. That doesn't mean that everybody else has fallen short in some way."

Haywood laughed. "I've not taken any offence, Mr Green. But you would be a crowd of mugs if you hadn't listened to what I had to say. By the same token, I'd be a mug not to pay attention to ideas, however strange, that emanate from your side of the fence."

"I'm glad of that. Had the boyo got anything in his pockets to interest us?"

"Ah! That's one of the things I wanted to mention to you as officers in charge of the case. Boyce's pockets were emptied by

Sergeant Watson when the lad was put in the cell. The contents have not been released to me yet."

"Why ever not?"

"Because I haven't so far asked for them, and I suppose Sergeant Watson was in too much of a flap to send them with the body to the mortuary. Don't worry. The order of things has gone a bit astray. Usually I get the body and everything attached to it all at once. Fortunately those who die in police cells—where, naturally, they have been stripped of most possessions—are enough of a rarity to get the drill a bit fouled up."

Masters turned to Betty Prior. "Is Sergeant Watson still on duty?"

"No, Chief, he was due off at four."

"Please find Mr Snell and tell him that Professor Haywood would like to examine the contents of Boyce's pockets."

"Bring them down here, Chief?"

"No, we'll come up."

After the girl had gone, Masters turned to Reed. "I'd like you and Berger to start making enquiries about thefts from chemists' shops."

"Recently, Chief?"

"During the last six months. Concentrate in this area. Regional H.Q. should be able to help you. I want to know when, how, what and who."

"Particularly if any of this sodium aurothiomalate has gone missing?"

"Or anything like it containing gold."

As Masters, Green and Haywood got to their feet, the professor said: "You know, Masters, I don't think your average thief would break in and pinch those ampoules. What I mean is, they are not the sort of drugs which attract thieves."

"Unless the person who broke in knew exactly what he was after," said Green. "A knowledgeable bastard."

"That would presuppose," countered Haywood, "that this killing was premeditated and planned with a great degree of care over a period of time. I find it difficult to believe that anybody would go to such trouble to kill a youth—a bit of a yob of a youth—but still a youth and, I suppose, a relatively harmless one who, in the scheme of things, was a comparatively unimportant hunk of humanity. Who would go to the trouble of robbing a chemist's shop for toxic substances when a clout with an iron bar would have done the job just as effectively?"

"Quite right, Professor," said Masters. "My idea exactly. But . . ."

"But what?"

"I asked you where this gold salt could be obtained. You mentioned three sources. A chemist's shop, a doctor's surgery or the home of somebody who has been given a prescription."

"I should have added a hospital pharmacy, a drug manufacturer's store or a drug wholesaler's stock."

Masters acknowledged these additions and said: "We could also consider theft during transit from factory to wholesaler or from wholesaler to retailer."

"That, of course. It is amazing how many alternatives there are when one comes to count them up."

"And all must be considered or eliminated. The first I have discarded is that which presupposes that a rheumatoid arthritic patient was the source. I cannot believe that a drug which is used so sparingly and so cautiously would be prescribed and supplied in an amount approaching that which you found in Boyce's body. You told us that the maximum dose for a month for one person would be fifty milligrams and that only rarely. Yet you found two thousand milligrams in Boyce's body—a supply sufficient for forty months at top whack. What doctor would ever write a prescription for that much for one person to keep in reserve against monthly jabs?"

Haywood scratched his head in perplexity. "It does sound so unlikely as to be not worth considering," he admitted.

"How many family doctors would carry that much on their premises?"

"Only a dispensing doctor would stock any at all."

"And how many dispensing doctors are there these days?"

"About ten per cent."

"One in ten and all in rural areas, I believe?"

"That's right. Far away from a High Street chemist."

"And you suggest that such doctors would not have two thousand milligrams of sodium aurothiomalate?"

"Highly unlikely. It is too expensive. No G.P. would tie up so much money in slow moving stock. Besides, gold is, as I told you, light-sensitive, and so it is an even guess that its shelf life is relatively limited—compared with many other drugs, that is."

"So we have also eliminated doctors. Now, what about hospital dispensaries?"

"Ah! There the picture could be very different. For one thing, they tend to buy in bulk, to save money. In fact, in lots of areas, several hospitals will join together to do contract buying on more favourable terms."

"Professor, nobody has a greater admiration for the medical profession than I have. And my regard extends to hospitals. All my experience and observation of them at many a tricky moment tells me that we're damned lucky to have such generally fine institutions. But having said that, I must confess that I have often had cause to criticise what I will call the bureaucratic side of hospitals. In other words, I would never think of criticising their medical expertise or their immediate care of patients, but I have personally encountered small—but nevertheless irritating—examples of administrative crassness."

"So have I," rumbled Green. "Doris—my missus—had to attend an afternoon clinic. Her appointment was for three o'clock. So were half a dozen other people's—all to see the same man. I was with her, of course, and I wasn't best pleased at being wheeled into the presence at nearly half past five.

"However, that wasn't what riled me. The doctor told Doris to attend the path lab two days later—for a blood test—and to arrange to see him again a fortnight later.

"So far, so good. I wasn't going to criticise a hard-working consultant physician who'd restored my missus to full health and had taken a load of trouble over doing it. If his consultations ran on a bit overtime, that was fine by me. He was doing a good job. But when we got downstairs to the desk where we had to make the appointment, we found nobody on duty. They'd packed up and gone home. Now, in the police, we'd make sure that as long as the clinics were open and going strong, that desk would be manned.

"But that wasn't all. The doctor had given us the path lab card. The place opened at half past eight in the morning. I got Doris there in such good time, we were first. A nice little lass in the office took our card, and recorded the details. Then other people started trooping in. At nine the technicians started work. But was Doris called first? Not on your N.H.S.! The nice little lass had piled up the cards as she got them, and the lab assistants were taking them off the top. It was a case of first come, last served, and Doris had eaten nothing nor taken a drink—not even water—since six the night before—as instructed. It took me some time to realise what had happened. I wanted to play merry hell, but Doris didn't want me to—for her sake. So I made a mild little protest which was ignored not because it was invalid, but because the nice little lass said that everybody was always complaining about everything and if I didn't like it I could go to another hospital."

"I think I know what you are going to say," said Haywood. "That in institutions where there are such obvious and easily remedied loopholes in administration as the ones you have encountered yourselves, you must consider the possibility of there being other areas of slackness—like the security of dispensaries and watertight accountability of drugs."

"Not necessarily that," said Masters. "The pharmacists are professional men and know their jobs, just as do the doctors and nurses on the wards. But hospitals are big places and dispensaries are probably overworked. I don't think that in many of them the pharmacist delivers drugs himself to each ward. There are messengers of one sort or another who leave loaded trolleys in corridors while they carry supplies from them into wards. Maybe it's against the rules, but it happens, particularly with drugs which are not scheduled as dangerous poisons."

"So?"

"There were two thousand milligrams in Boyce's body. To me, that sounds like a pharmacist's stock or a hospital rheumatology department's supply." Masters got to his feet.

As they moved out to find Betty Prior and Boyce's belongings,

Haywood asked: "So you've eliminated everybody except those two sources?"

"Not eliminated completely. But shall we say I have chosen to concentrate on them for the moment?"

Betty and Snell were waiting for them. The contents of Boyce's pockets were spread on the typist's table behind the desk.

"I can see why Watson didn't bother to let me have them," said Haywood. "There isn't even a handkerchief."

"But there is this," said Masters, picking up the white plastic stopper and handing it to Haywood.

"And what would you expect me to do with that?"

"Nothing, Professor."

"You mean it is likely to tell you more than it is me."

Masters took the stopper from him. It was made of polythene—a hollow cylinder with three lateral ridges to give it the grip of a conventional cork, and a round disc top, three-sixteenths of an inch thick and milled to make removal from a bottle easier.

"Why would a youth keep a cheap article like that? It has a certain amount of aesthetic appeal, I suppose, and I won't suggest that because Boyce was a loutish youth he had no appreciation of form or materials. In fact, something of this sort must have caused him to keep the stopper. But as with all such little peccadilloes, he would soon have tired of so useless an article. And that is what this stopper says to me. He came across it only a matter of hours before his death, otherwise he would have rid himself of it, because it really is a lumpy sort of article to carry in the rather skimpy pockets of skin-tight jeans."

Green took out a crumpled packet of cigarettes and helped himself. "It's an amateur wine-maker's bung, isn't it?" he asked as he struck a match.

"Is it? Exclusively, I mean?" asked Haywood.

Snell said, "I'd say it was, sir. Not many professional bottlers would use that. They've started to use plastic tops to ordinary corks in cheaper wines, but I've never seen an all-polythene closure on any wine I've bought."

"I think Mr Snell is right," said Masters. "I know very little about wine making, but I do happen to know that for the insertion of an ordinary cork, a corking gun is needed. I would have thought that very few amateur wine-makers would go to the expense of buying items of equipment like corking guns when stoppers like this are available. The advantages are obvious. They can be inserted by hand; I imagine they can be sterilised to be used more than once; and my guess is that individually they couldn't be all that much dearer than corks."

"It all adds up," said Green.

"What does?" asked Snell.

Masters turned to the local man. "Your people thought Boyce was drunk when they brought him in, despite subsequent assertions that he had drunk very little beer. The truth—as found by Professor Haywood—is that Boyce had drunk a full bottle of white wine—presumably before his visit to the pub to top up with beer."

"I'm pleased to know that, sir."

"I'm sure you are. What we were in fact discussing was what sort of wine was it, and where did Boyce get it. The professor suggested cheap plonk. We have been speculating on whether it could have been home-made white wine. The finding of the stopper seems to support our belief that it was of the home-made variety."

"I'd go along with that," said Snell, "without hearing the pros and cons. A chap like Boyce wouldn't buy wine from an off-licence. The only time he would drink it would be if he could knock it off—from some house he'd broken into."

"Right, lad," agreed Green.

"Well," said Haywood, "I must be going. It's been a pleasure meeting you and your merry men, Masters. I hope we'll bump into each other again before you leave."

"I'm sure we shall. Thank you very much for coming and talking to us. Many in your line of business are content with providing just a written report."

Haywood grinned. "Strictly speaking, remember, my written report is the coroner's property. You know by law he had to come and view the body before I started the autopsy and he was careful to remind me that copies were not to be given to anyone else without his permission. He fully intends you to have one, of course, but I thought that in the circumstances you shouldn't be expected to work blind. I've done as he said, but there is nothing to prevent me coming to talk to you."

"As I said, we appreciate it."

"I've enjoyed talking to you. Cheerio."

After the professor had gone, Masters turned to Green. "I think I would like to go back to the hotel for a bath. That recreation room is pretty sticky in weather like this."

"I shall have a bath, too," said Green. "I wonder if the barman will mind providing me with a large, iced drink."

"For before or after the bath?" asked Berger.

"Before, after and with," answered Green.

Masters and Green met by arrangement, in the hotel bar, at seven o'clock.

Reed was there. "No thefts from retail pharmacies where gold salts were lifted, Chief. No wholesalers either. Regional H.Q. has had no reports of any sort from hospital pharmacies for years. If there are any losses, they are either covered up or ignored."

"Thank you. So now what are we left with?"

"Quite a lot of good drinking time before dinner," said Green.

"You've already had one before and one in your bath," accused Berger.

"True, lad, but they were only to whet—or wet—my appetite in preparation for the dirty great pint you're about to buy me."

"Buy your own. It's not my round."

"I've already bought a round."

"For yourself."

"I was the only one there because I usually bath alone. But it still constitutes a round."

"Allow me," said Masters, handing Reed a note. "Make them all long and cold, please."

Green sat down in one of the chairs at the window table. "George," he said, "while Haywood was speaking, I could almost see your old mind linking rheumatoid arthritis with Miss Foulger, and home-made wine with Miss Foulger, and Boyce with Miss Foulger, and a mysterious break-in connected with wine belonging to Miss Foulger . . ."

"You were obviously doing the same."

Green grimaced. "It stuck out a mile."

"But?"

"Lots of buts, chum. Too much poison for one. We don't know whether she has ever had gold treatment for another. We have nothing to connect her with Boyce except the chance meeting in court, for a third."

"We're swinging about a bit, Chief," said Berger. "We were looking at the tramp first, now we're looking at the magistrate."

"Wrong as usual, lad. We were just saying we weren't looking at the magistrate."

"So who are we looking at?"

"Not who, lad. What!" said Green appreciatively as Reed put a foaming glass of cold beer in front of him.

"You mean all you're interested in is a pint of wallop."

"Not at all." Green took a deep, noisy gulp, set the tankard down and wiped his mouth with the back of his hand. "Bonanza," he added.

"What the devil are you talking about now?"

"Eldorado, Yukon, gold-rush!"

"You mean we are seeking gold? We know that much."

"Then why ask, lad?"

"Because we were talking about people."

"You were. You'll notice His Nibs isn't saying much. And why? Because he's cross. As cross as two sticks."

"The Chief? Angry?"

"Of course he is. We've spent today pottering, because we didn't know what killed Boyce."

"We did know. Poison."

"But not which poison, so we couldn't go looking for it. As I said we've spent today pottering, and His Nibs doesn't take kindly to that. He is of the opinion that Haywood should have had the answer last night."

"Are you, Chief?"

"Most assuredly," said Masters. "If you were to ask him, Haywood would say that it took him a long time to find and then to blame gold for Boyce's death. But even he admits that so long a delay is not attributable to the fact that the presence of gold was hard to confirm but to the fact that it was unexpected. In other words, he didn't work from a knowledge of Boyce's physical reaction to the poison, but to a knowledge of the frequency of use of the more common poisons."

"How do you mean, Chief?"

"He did a blood test straight away. We know that, because he was able, yesterday afternoon, to inform the Chief Constable that Boyce had died from a massive shortage of blood platelets."

"Thrombocytopenia?"

"Yes. I know there are a good few substances which cause blood disorders, and of these, gold is one of the biggest culprits. But because he could not envisage gold being used for this purpose, he pushed it aside and tested for everything else before he turned to it. In other words, it should have been high on the list, not last."

Reed grimaced. "So we have to concentrate on finding the source of the gold—the means by which Boyce was murdered—before we can turn to thinking of who had the opportunity and motive?"

"Right, lad," said Green. "And as that seems to be the first priority, it is only fair to say that we should have concentrated on that today. Unlike Haywood, we'd prefer to put first things first, however unlikely."

"You're saying that we've wasted today?"

"No," said Masters before Green could reply. "We haven't wasted today, but we haven't exactly rooted up any trees."

"So what do we do now, Chief?"

"Have dinner," said Green. Having disposed of Reed, he turned to Masters. "Would you like me to tackle them? I'll probably get more out of them than you."

"Yes, please. Take Berger."

"To do what?" asked Berger. "What the devil are we talking about?"

Green shook his head sadly. "After all this time, and you've still not learned to mind read." Before Berger could intervene, he went on: "We're going to find those other two young yobs and ask them a few questions."

"And about time, too."

"You think so?" asked Masters mildly.

"Yes, Chief. I'd have talked to them first thing this morning."

"And asked them what?"

"Where they'd all been after leaving the magistrates' court."

"And what answer would you have expected to get?"

"How do I know, Chief? But something."

"You're sure? What if they said they'd been nowhere except into a pizza parlour and then the pub? What good would that have done you?"

"Well, Chief . . ."

"Feel for the bedpost, lad," advised Green. "By waiting for Haywood's report, we know that Boyce drank a full bottle of vin blanc. It's not the sort of stuff a character like him buys for himself. And, as various little things like the bottle stopper suggest the wine was home-made, we are left wondering which amateur vintner brewed the stuff and then, having done so, gave a bottle to Boyce."

"Nobody would give him it, judging by what we've heard," said Berger. "People just don't show generosity to young tearaways like him."

"Quite. So where and how did he get the wine—seeing we reckon he didn't buy it and he wasn't given it?"

"He nicked it, of course."

"Of course? And when did you reach that decision?"

"After the Professor told us . . ."

"Not this morning?"

"No."

"But you think that this morning we should have sought out Boyce's two pals—pals who went everywhere with him—and asked them where they went on Tuesday? You were actually proposing to ask two youths who, a few hours before, had been up in front of the magistrates where they had been? I suppose you think they would have confessed that they had accompanied their pal on a break-in where he had stolen a bottle of wine? Just like that? They would have confessed and put themselves straight in the nick for a double sentence apiece?"

109

"Well, no. But they seemed the obvious people to approach first."

"So His Nibs and I were wrong to decide against doing just that when we discussed it last night?"

"Not as it's turned out, you weren't, because now you've got a lot of ammunition to use. You know most of the story. They'll think you know it all and . . ."

"And what?"

"They'll cave in."

"Let's hope so. Now, whose round is it?"

"Yours. What are you going to be doing, Chief, while the D.C.I. and I are seeing these yobbos?"

Masters smiled. "You should be able to guess."

"Should I?" Berger's face advertised his concentration. "Oh, I get you. If I thought his boy friends should be seen first, then his girlfriend should have been next on the list."

"Quite right."

"But what do you hope to get there, Chief?"

"Probably nothing. But I might be able to mend a few fences."

"In that case," said Green, "we ought to be fortifying ourselves with a few piles of food."

"Steaks?" asked Reed. "You know, STAKES?"

"Pick at a few bits and pieces?"

"Shovel it in, you mean."

"Enough," said Masters. "Let's have dinner now, so that we can get some work done afterwards."

Chapter 6

MASTERS AND REED decided to walk to Watson's house, leaving
the car free for Green and Berger who would have the less precise
job of tracking down Lawson and Mobb.

Before he set out, Masters phoned his wife. Masters had great
regard for Wanda's commonsense and wisdom over matters such
as the one he was about to take in hand.

After she had been given a brief outline of the problem, Wanda
said: "It will all depend on the girlie's state of mind, George.
Nobody should try to force her to come to any particular decision.
If she's sensible, she'll work it out for herself. Only if she asks for
help should it be given, but make sure she realises that the help is
there should she feel the need to ask for it."

"She's only seventeen, poppet."

"I know it sounds pathetic, George, but even at that age she will
have at least the beginnings of the feelings of a mature woman. Her
mind may still be immature. You can guide the latter if needs be.
On no account must you try to tamper with the former."

"Understood."

"I'm sure you'll deal with it very successfully, but I can't quite
see why you should concern yourself. You're there to investigate a
murder, not to do social work."

"The need may not arise for me to do anything. But Tom
Watson is a decent chap and just the sort of paternal sergeant the
force needs and the public needs. I'd like to help him if I can."

"He isn't the first decent man whose teenage daughter has gone
off the rails. We women do it quite a lot. Remember, I'm not
entirely without experience myself."

"So I'm to steer clear?"

"I didn't say that. But please use a great deal of caution otherwise you could do more harm than good."

"I'll tread warily."

"And, George . . ."

"Yes, poppet?"

"If there's anything I can do . . ."

"Practically, you mean?"

"That, of course. But I also meant . . . well, I know one or two people in the adoption world."

"Thank you. We'll see how it goes."

"How are we going to find Lawson and Mobb?" demanded Berger as he and Green left the dinner table. "They could be anywhere."

"Use your loaf, lad," grunted Green. "Young Sutcliffe has been keeping an eye on them these last few weeks. Get on to the blower. Ask the nick for his home number and ask him for likely places and how to get to them. If he offers to guide us, accept, but don't put the idea into his head—much. Do that while I go get myself some more fags and be down at the car with the answers in ten minutes' time."

The outcome of Berger's conversations was that within twenty minutes they were waiting outside the police station for Constable Sutcliffe. He joined them there, dressed in slacks and a modern shirt which had no collar and reminded Green of the workmen of his day who wore just such items, but usually with a front collar stud to fasten the gaping neck.

Sutcliffe suggested that the best idea in his opinion was to call at the homes of the two youths to make sure they were out and about. If no definite news of their whereabouts was forthcoming from either of these sources, then he, Sutcliffe, was pretty sure he could track them down at one of their haunts. The suggestion appealed to Green, who sat back in his usual seat, lit a cigarette, and appeared to take no further interest in the search.

However, when the car reached Mobb's home, it was Green who knocked on the door. The house was one of a terrace built in the early fifties. As they were situated on a slight rise, no two were on the same level. There was a difference of about a foot in the roof levels as they climbed the hill. They had obviously been thrown up in a hurry with little thought and less taste.

"Mr Mobb?"

The man was dressed as if he fully intended stepping out for what was left of the evening.

"Yes?"

"I would like to speak to your son, Ted."

"Well you can't. For one thing he isn't here, and for another I don't let strange . . ."

"Police," said Green forcefully. "Scotland Yard, to be more precise. So stop the fond father act and tell me where the lad is."

"Scotland Yard? What's Ted done?"

"Done? You knew he was up in court on Tuesday, didn't you?"

"Of course I did."

"You also know that Norman Boyce who was charged with him has since died, don't you?"

"I knew he'd been murdered, probably by you lot."

"Murdered is right. But don't you think a lad whose pal gets murdered should be questioned by police?"

"I suppose so."

"Then why the panic? Why ask me what he's done?"

"Because I don't want my lad to die mysteriously in a police cell."

"He won't see a police cell if you tell me where I can find him to ask him some questions. But if I don't find him I'll have him brought in."

"I don't know where he is."

"What about his mother? Does she know?"

"She's out at bingo."

"I see. Now, Mr Mobb, I'll give you a word of advice. It strikes me you let young Ted do much as he likes."

"He's over eighteen."

"Right, and I don't suggest you keep him at home like a child, but take a bit of interest in him and what he does. Believe you me, mate, it'll save you and your missus a lot of aggro in the future."

"What do you mean by that?"

"Now don't get me wrong about this, but your Ted got off very lightly for a chap who's done a break-in. Right?"

"Yeah."

"Well, there have been a lot of other break-ins round here that the local cops haven't managed to get a line on yet. But if they do, and your lad was in on any of those, he'll be for the high jump." He held up his hand to stop Mobb interrupting. "Conversely, if there are any more in the future—well, you know how it is—the local cops now reckon they know where to look. So your Ted's in a tricky situation if he puts a foot wrong. So take an interest, mate. At least ask him where he's going at night. Even if he doesn't tell you the truth you'll be showing him you know he exists."

"You've no right . . ."

"I've every right, Mr Mobb. In fact, I could insist on coming in and turning your house over."

"What for?"

"We're looking for a few things we know about and probably a few we don't. Murder cases play hell with the lives of those involved."

"But my lad isn't involved."

"How do you know? Have you asked him?"

"No."

"Are you a betting man, Mr Mobb?"

"Now and again. Why?"

"Would you like to put a fiver on your Ted not knowing something he hasn't told you about this case? Or make it a tenner, if you like."

Mobb opened his mouth and closed it again without replying. Green said: "Well, we're off to find him. Do you want to be there when we talk to him?"

"I can't, can I? I said I'd have a jar with this bloke tonight."

"I hope you enjoy it, Mr Mobb."

When Green rejoined the car, Sutcliffe said: "You don't half talk to them, Mr Green."

"You heard?"

"At a distance of about six feet?" asked Berger. "We got it all." He turned to Sutcliffe. "Which way?"

"Lawson's mother is a widow," said Sutcliffe. "I've never

114

spoken to her, but I hear she's a decent-living woman."

So Green was surprised when the door of the council flat opened and a woman of no more than forty, dressed in clean, well-pressed slacks and striped open-neck shirt replied, in answer to his question, that she was Mrs Lawson.

"Eric is beyond me," she said. "I go out to work, you see. I've got a good job in an office, with a good boss. I need it, to keep us going. But I'm not here in the daytime, and Eric is. He's out of work with too much time on his hands. If he'd met decent lads since he finished school he'd be decent himself. As it is, he met two undesirables and he's gone the wrong way."

"Not a strong character then, your Eric?"

"As weak as water, really. He's more frightened of his pals than he is of me. My fault, I suppose. I lost his father when he was very small and I probably didn't give him the necessary amount of backbone."

Green shrugged. "It's been tough on you, and tough on the lad."

"Thanks for appreciating that. I suppose you want to question him about this Boyce business?"

"Yes. Has he said anything about it?"

"He hasn't even mentioned it."

"I see. When we see him we'll try not to be too hard on him."

"Is he involved in some way?"

"Not with the murder itself maybe, but he may be able to tell us Boyce's movements. You can be present when we speak to him if you like."

"Do you think I'd better be there? What I mean is, I ought to be there, but won't he be less inhibited if I'm not there?"

"Search me, love. But I'll tell you what. If I reckon he'll be better with you holding his hand, I'll get in touch and you can come running."

"Thank you. That seems the best arrangement."

"And you don't know where he is?"

"I did ask him where he was going."

"But all he said was, 'Out'. Is that it?"

"That's it."

Sutcliffe led them to a youth club, a billiards hall and then to a public house, at all of which he made brief enquiries. Then finally they pulled up at a brightly lit pin-ball machine arcade. Sutcliffe disappeared inside and returned within a minute.

"They're here, sir."

"Doing what?"

"Mobb is playing a table. Lawson's watching."

"We can't talk in there. The noise would drown a couple of dozen panotropes."

"Shall I go in and get them, sir?"

Never one to ask others to tackle what he was unprepared to do himself, Green got heavily from the car. "Not you, lad. You're not supposed to be involved in this. Just point them out to us and then sit in the car."

Sutcliffe led the way through the wide doorway and chose an alley between two rows of machines. The pin-tables were ranked against the back wall. "The two playing the third table from the left, sir. Mobb's the one playing, with his back to us."

"Thanks."

Berger followed Green. There were not many customers and, as far as Berger could tell, their progress was unremarked, though they were an unlikely couple for such a place.

"Ted and Eric, isn't it?" said Green, coming up quietly behind the unsuspecting Mobb.

"Who wants to know?" asked Mobb, looking round.

"We already know, lad," said Green. "You look a bit like your dad. But he's better washed."

"Listen, grandad . . ."

"Ted!" warned Lawson.

"No, you listen," said Berger, big, young and strong. "Listen and listen hard. You're talking to a Detective Chief Inspector from Scotland Yard, sonny, and that spells trouble for anybody who's sassy and unco-operative, particularly young tearaways who are known house-breakers. So let's watch it, shall we?"

"Cops! You're all alike."

"No, lad," said Green. "We're not. For instance, if we'd been here you'd have been inside now for those first four or five jobs you pulled. You may think you fooled the local cops, but not us. And now we've got you for the last one."

"What last one?"

"The one where your pal Boyce nicked the bottle of vino, chummy."

"It wasn't us . . ." began Lawson.

"Can it, Eric."

"Don't worry, son," replied Green. "We've got it all. And we're going to be rather hard on you two for telling a lot of lies to that reporter. Policemen don't like yobs who tell lies about them. So now you know the score."

"You've no evidence."

"Oh, I reckon we can get it. We've only got to give your boots to the scientists. They'll tell us lots of things."

"Like what?"

"Fine bits of glass embedded in the soles. Wine stains on the plastic. It's easy these days."

Green seemed to have found the key. Mobb said: "It hadn't anything to do with us. Norm did it all himself."

"Blaming it on the dead lad, are you?"

"It's true."

"Right, come along, we want to talk to you."

"I'm not going anywhere," said Mobb belligerently. "You haven't got a warrant to arrest me."

"Quite right," said Green. "I haven't got one. But you're making the same mistake lots of others like you make when you think a copper can't feel your collar unless he's got a warrant to wave in your face. I can take you in now."

"You haven't got a charge."

"Oh, yes, I have, lad. One you won't like."

"What?"

"Suspicion of murder."

"I haven't murdered anybody."

"I hope not. I just said suspicion of murder. And take it from me, boy, if I deliver you to the Colesworth nick, the fuzz there will make absolutely sure you two spend the night banged up in the cell where your pal died two nights ago. That'll be their idea of a joke."

Lawson, who had been very quiet, now asked: "When you said you wanted to talk to us, sir, did that mean you weren't going to arrest us?"

"That's exactly what I meant, only your pal here seems intent on making it hard for himself—and you!"

"Suspicion of murder!" sneered Mobb. "No way!"

"If you're so sure," said Berger, "why don't you want to talk?"

"Talk to the pigs? You must think I'm crackers."

"That's exactly what we think," said Green. "Now, lad, you've one last chance. Either come and talk or risk arrest. And before you answer, let me promise you this. If you choose to talk, I shall tell you just why I could arrest you on suspicion of murder, with every chance of making it stick. And just in case you still want to play it the hard way, we two are not alone. We have a little bit of help all round the building. In fact, your friend Constable Sutcliffe is the one right outside the door. He came with me in my car. Now, lad, the choice is yours. Come and talk or stay in a cell overnight."

"Let's do what he wants, Ted. It can't do any harm."

Mobb turned to Green. "Come? Where to?"

"Well now, what about having a cosy chat in one of your homes? Mrs Lawson won't mind, will she? And I know she isn't out tonight, while Mr and Mrs Mobb are both out."

"At our house?"

"Yes, Eric. You see, lad, when I promised you a chat, that's exactly what I meant. Nothing more. And if we're just going to talk, well, your mum being there and the familiar surroundings will give you a bit of confidence, won't it? And maybe we'll be lucky enough to get a cup of coffee."

"She doesn't like me," said Mobb.

"Who's she, lad? The cat's mother?"

Mobb didn't reply. Green turned to Berger. "Nip on ahead, Sergeant, and tell Constable Sutcliffe to go along to the corner and tell the local sergeant to stand his other three men down. Warn Sutcliffe to get back to the car sharpish as I don't want to hang about."

Berger replied with a straight face: "Right, sir," and then went off ahead. By the time Green and his two charges reached the door of the amusement arcade, Sutcliffe was speeding towards the nearest corner.

"In you get," ordered Green. "And leave room for the constable." He ushered them into the back seat, and Berger had the surprise of seeing his superior take the—to him—unaccustomed front passenger seat. After a minute or so, Sutcliffe came galloping back.

"All fixed, sir. The sergeant's withdrawing the other three."

"Good. Get in with the lads. There's plenty of room for three at the back of this barouche."

The door was opened by a woman in her early forties. Masters liked the look of her. Wholesome. The sort of woman he imagined Tom Watson would marry—with a nice unlined face, a good—if comfortable—figure and a youthful neatness of dress that suggested a tidy mind, a tidy home and a tidy bit of comfort to go with it.

"Mrs Watson?"

"Yes."

"I am Detective Chief Superintendent Masters, and this is Detective Sergeant Reed. Would it be convenient to have a few words with you and your daughter, please?"

A faint flicker of worry showed in her kindly eyes. "Tom is at home, Mr Masters."

"All the better. He isn't expecting me, but I thought I would like to call for a chat. Is your daughter in, too?"

"Yes. But I shouldn't be keeping you here on the doorstep . . ."

As they stepped into the hall, Sergeant Watson appeared from a room on the right. "Hello, sir! Is something the matter?" He sounded nervous.

"No, Tom, but I thought I'd better have a word with your daughter—if it is convenient, of course."

"She's upstairs. I'll fetch her," volunteered Mrs Watson.

"Do that, Freda," said her husband, "while Mr Masters tells me why he thinks he'd like to speak to Pam." As his wife went upstairs, he led the way into the room. "Now, sir, what's it all about? I don't like my girl tangling with the police—particularly at your level."

"I don't really know why I want to see your daughter. I could claim, of course, that I would be failing in my duty if I were not to interview one of Boyce's closest companions. But I'm not claiming that."

Tom Watson suddenly reddened angrily. "Just one moment, Mr Masters. You told me that you had virtually eliminated young Sutcliffe and myself as suspects."

"True enough. I did say words to that effect."

"So you are looking for somebody else."

"That's right."

"And now you've come to see my Pam! Why, you . . ."

"Hold it, Tom! Hold it!" said Reed, stepping in between Watson and Masters. "You've got it all wrong."

"Have I? I know how he works. Don't forget I had a session with him myself today. He can prove you're a criminal for not seeing a coincidence in an Incident Book. What do you think he could do to my girl?"

"Stand aside, Reed," said Masters quietly. As the detective sergeant did so, Masters continued: "You're right, Sergeant Watson. I could suggest that your daughter gave Boyce a dose of poison early on Tuesday evening and he took it because he would never suspect any action of hers."

"There you are! You see?"

"Further, I could suggest that your daughter adopted the classic attitude the following morning of claiming that some other person had murdered Boyce—namely you, her father."

"You could make black sound like white."

"A father with whom she had had a bitter argument only a few hours earlier and whom she—temporarily, at any rate—wasn't too fond of at the time."

"You make me sick."

"But I could make out an even stronger case against Mrs Watson. The mother exacting revenge for what had happened to her daughter. And poison is a woman's weapon. And so on and so on."

"You've got a twisted mind."

"I don't think so. I didn't come here to suggest either of those solutions to my problems."

"No?"

"If you recall, it was you who suggested that was the reason for my visit. As a matter of fact, it never occurred to me to suspect either your wife or your daughter. I came simply to visit you and your family."

"You asked for Pam by name."

"She is the ostensible reason for my visit. But I did ask if it would be convenient to see her. I didn't force my way in, or, indeed, con my way in. However, I am quite willing to go and leave you in peace if you wish me to."

"And I suppose you'd put your own interpretation on it if I did ask you to go?"

"Naturally. I should say I'd just met a normally decent man who, because he is so unhappy, is suspicious of everybody and everything."

"You'll be trying to tell me you understand next." Watson sounded less belligerent, more bitter.

"In a way. You could say not so much understanding as fellow-feeling. You see, I have a son. He's only a little chap yet, nowhere near as old as your Pam, but I confess to you, Tom, that if anybody were to harm him or lead him astray . . . well, I suppose I might stop just short of murder, but not much. And as to what my thoughts might be at such a time . . ."

"You mean you'd be glad if whoever had done it was to die in a police cell?"

"In a police cell or wherever, I'd still be glad."

"By God, I think you mean it."

"He does," said Reed. "And Mr Green would be worse. He's the boy's godfather and he and his missus regard him as something . . . something holy, you might say. So don't run away with the idea that the D.C.I. will be gunning for your daughter either."

"You swear this is true?"

"I've told you," growled Reed. "What do you want? Me to write it on my shirt-front in blood?"

Watson was suddenly deflated. He sat down like a tired man

who has fought hard all day and failed. "They'll be down in a minute," he said. "Freda will have told Pam to wash her face and comb her hair."

"We'll still go if you want us to."

"No, sir. Sit down, please. I'd like you to see her."

"Any beer in the house, Tom?" asked Reed.

"A couple of cans, maybe. Do you want them?"

"I'll slip out for some. There was an off-licence open just down the road. P'raps he's got some in a cold cabinet."

"Aye. Maybe."

Reed let himself out, and a moment or two later Mrs Watson appeared. "I thought I heard the front door."

"Just Sergeant Reed slipping out for some beer, Mrs Watson. And this is Pam, is it?" Masters, who had got to his feet, held out his hand to the girl. "Your father told me you were pretty. He should have said you were a smasher."

The hand was limp, and though Pamela was a pleasant enough girl, she seemed rather insipid to Masters. Watson's swan was by no means a goose, but Masters sensed a weakness in the character. He mentally chided himself for doing so. Pam was still a school-girl, she had recently discovered she was pregnant, and less than forty-eight hours earlier she had heard that the father of her expected child was dead. He reckoned that any woman—mature or not—would need a bit of stamina to stand up to such blows. Always assuming that she knew the import of events.

"Mummy said you want to ask me some questions."

Masters smiled. "Sit down, Pam. Alongside me here on the sofa, then your mother and father can have an armchair apiece."

"These questions . . . ?" she said as she obeyed his instructions. "They're not . . . ?"

"Harrowing? Harrassing?"

She nodded.

Masters paused a moment, looking at her before replying. Then he replied: "What would you say if I said they were?"

Masters heard Freda Watson gasp, but he didn't take his eyes from the girl's face.

She made no reply, so he went on: "I'll tell you what you should say, shall I? You should say you've done nothing criminal. You may have acted foolishly perhaps, but not criminally. So you should say straight away that I can ask any questions I like, because you've nothing to hide."

She paused to think for a moment and then said: "You mean I should separate the two things and not mix them up?"

"Right."

"What two things?" asked Watson.

"Oh, dad! Mr Masters means Norman's death and the baby."

"Oh!"

"Two separate problems," said Masters, "to be dealt with separately. So . . . I'll deal with Norman's death and then we'll deal with the baby together. Will that suit?"

She nodded her assent.

"Good. Well, there's only one real question I want to ask you about Mr Boyce. Ready?"

"Yes."

"Can you ever remember him buying a bottle of wine or even drinking wine at any time?"

She stared at him in amazement. "Is that all?"

"Yes."

"He never bought wine. He couldn't afford it, could he? And he wouldn't have bought it in a pub or at the Pizza House because he would think that only other people would have wine."

"Other people?"

"People like . . . well, like you. People with money. Not the working class like him."

"Thank you."

"And what does that tell you, sir?" asked Watson.

"Quite a lot. You won't have heard the pathologist's report, but I can tell you that Boyce drank a full bottle of white wine before his two beers on the night he died."

"No wonder Sutcliffe thought he was drunk."

"A reasonable mistake. The trouble is, the wine was poisoned."

Watson leaned forward. "I get it, sir. You want to know where the wine came from."

"Obviously. And if your daughter can assure me that Norman

123

Boyce is unlikely to have bought it, then I must consider the other ways in which it could have come into his possession."

Watson grunted. It was obvious to Masters that the sergeant had his own ideas about this, but didn't want to say in front of his daughter that Boyce had, more than likely, stolen the bottle.

"At this moment," Masters continued, "D.C.I. Green and Sergeant Berger are interviewing Messrs Lawson and Mobb to discover if they know the source of the wine."

Watson sat forward in his chair. "You're not going to get me twice with the same trick, Mr Masters. Miss Foulger's wine store was vandalised some time before she got home last Tuesday. I'll add two and two together and tell you here and now that it was from there that young Boyce got his wine—or I'm a Dutchman."

Masters grinned at him. "My thoughts exactly, Tom, but . . ."

He was interrupted by the ringing of the doorbell.

Watson got to his feet. "Aye, there's always a but. That'll be Sergeant Reed. I'll go let him in."

Reed came in with a plastic carrier bag full of cans. "I hope you can drink iced lager, Mrs Watson." He looked round at Masters. "I brought a can of coke in case there was anybody here who doesn't drink lager."

Freda Watson said: "I'll get some glasses." As she left the room her husband turned to Masters. "You were saying there's always a but, sir."

"So I was. If young Boyce got his wine from Miss Foulger's outhouse, it presupposes first, that Miss Foulger had poisoned a bottle of wine; second, that she knew Boyce would come to steal it; and third, that he would choose that particular bottle from among however many were there."

"Unless," said Reed, "she had poisoned all the bottles."

"I'm not accepting that," said Masters, "on two counts. First, the amount of poison needed to treat even two bottles would have been so massive as to be prohibitive. Second, no wine lover would poison a whole rack of bottles on the offchance that some scally-wag will break in, steal one and drink it. The idea doesn't make sense."

"Then, in that case," said Pamela Watson, surprisingly,

"Norman must somehow have given Miss Foulger a hint that he was going to her home to get the wine."

"Logical," agreed Masters. "But is it probable?"

"I can't see Norman and old Miss Foulger sharing secrets, if that's what you mean. But couldn't somebody else have told her?"

"A third party, you mean? Somebody who overheard Boyce's plans and then split to Miss Foulger. Again, possible. I will make it my business to learn whether Miss Foulger returned to her home that day before she discovered and reported the breakage. But even if she did hear that Boyce was going after her wine, would she poison the wine to kill him? Wouldn't she just have moved it to greater safety inside her house, or called upon your father for protection? She is a magistrate, you know, and they are inclined to regard the local police as there just to do their bidding."

Pam opened her eyes wide. "Somebody poisoned the wine. And the same arguments could be used whoever it was who did it."

"Not quite true, Pam."

"Somebody had to know that Norman was going there. Then they had to know which bottle he would nick. Then they had to poison it," said the girl.

"At the moment," said Masters, "I'll not argue with you. But may I ask you another question concerning Norman Boyce?"

"If it's not too . . . you know . . ."

"Personal? I'm afraid it is a bit personal."

"Oh!"

"Did he know you were going to have a baby?"

"Yes."

"Did he accept that he was the father?"

"Of course."

"Unhesitatingly?"

"You mean did he try to say somebody else was? No, he didn't."

"What did he say exactly? Did he talk about your going through with it?"

She hung her head. "He wanted me to have an abortion."

"You didn't tell me that," said her mother.

"It's just too easy, isn't it?" said Watson bitterly.

Pam looked across at her father. "But isn't that why there is abortion these days? So that you don't have unwanted babies?"

Masters said quietly: "That's all I really came to ask. I think Pam is right. It might have been different if Boyce had not died and marriage had been a possibility so that the baby would have had a father."

Mrs Watson looked at him gratefully. "It solves the problem, doesn't it? Makes it a plausible solution, I mean?"

Masters nodded. He knew that Freda Watson didn't like the idea of abortion and yet, because it would literally remove a bar to the future happiness of her family, she would accept it. She was grateful her conscience could be at least partly salved by what he himself had said. He felt relief, because here, in this normally happy little family, he sensed that an air of hatred had been dissipated. Watson and his wife had hated Boyce, or his memory. They were pleased he was dead. Not that they would ever admit it to themselves. But they were pleased. And now that Pam, with no prompting, had chosen an abortion, the last remnants of Boyce's unwelcome intrusion into their world would be eradicated. Boyce's own expressed wish that the child should never be born which, or so it seemed, had apparently influenced Pam's decision was probably, in their view, the one decent act of his life. Now that things were settled, relief was flooding into their beings. Masters could not find it in his heart to blame them. In fact, he confessed to himself that it was with some such idea in mind—to achieve just this solution—that he had called on the Watsons. Vaguely, he had thought that his presence would create an atmosphere in which the three members of the family would talk to each other whereas otherwise each might fight shy of such a discussion. He had no means of knowing whether what he sensed was true, but he, too, felt that the Watsons were once again united. It pleased him.

Reed, as if realising the crisis was over, came across to pour the last of the coke from the tin into Pam's glass. "If I'm free tomorrow night," he said, "I'd like to come and listen to some of your records."

She looked up at him. "All you policemen are very nice," she said.

"That's right, love. Including your dad."

Mrs Lawson showed very little surprise when she answered the door and found Green once again on her doorstep.

"Me again, love," he said. "With company. This is Detective Sergeant Berger who's working with me. Then there's Constable Sutcliffe, your own lad, and young Ted Mobb."

"So I see. What's it all about?"

"I told you I wanted to talk to your Eric, didn't I? And I said I wouldn't mind if you were present. So now I've found him I've brought him home. I want a word with Ted, too, so I thought you wouldn't mind if I did it all together while you listen and make us a pot of tea or a mug of Nescaff."

"Come in. If that's what you want . . ."

"To get it all over and done with, love."

They trooped in, and she sat them round her dining table. Eric had to fetch two stools from the kitchen to accommodate them.

"Now," said Green, offering his packet of Kensitas to Mrs Lawson, "what we've got to do is to discover exactly where young Boyce went last Tuesday after leaving the court; and we want to know every word he said, as well."

"May I know why those two things are so important?"

"He got hold of a bottle of wine that contained poison. He drank it. It killed him. I want to know where he got it from. And these two young men are going to tell me, even though it means they have to admit to another crime."

"I'm saying nothing," said Mobb, reverting to his previous obstinacy.

"Oh yes you are, lad, or the night in the cells is on without any hesitation. I'm not going to run around trying to get information from people who don't know it, while all the time you have the answers. So, let's get on with it. You left the court by soon after eleven in the morning of Tuesday. What happened? Where did you go?"

"To a café," mumbled Eric. "For a coffee."

"Which one?"

"It's opposite the court. Across the road. You go down some steps into it."

"The Basement," said Sutcliffe. "I know it. It's not bad. A sort of transport place, but used mostly by council manual workers and the like. They wouldn't get any booze there. And they wouldn't be allowed to act the fool, either. There's always enough strong arm talent in there to stop any youngsters trying to cause trouble."

"What did you talk about?" asked Green.

"Him mostly," said Mobb, nodding at Sutcliffe. "How he hadn't managed to get us."

"So it was a self-congratulatory session, was it? Then what?"

"When we came out of there it was nearly dinnertime," said Eric.

"Go on."

"We didn't want to stay in that Basement place, so we came out and walked up the road."

"Where to?"

"Well, we went round that crescent place and along the road that runs into Albert Street."

"That's near the railway station," said Sutcliffe.

"Then what?"

"There's a pie place there."

"Where?"

"At the bottom of the station approach. You can eat them inside or take them away."

"You bought pies?"

"And chips. We had them there. Norm liked it because they cook curry and fry onions and it always smelt good to him."

"But you didn't like it?"

"Not much. It's only about as big as this room and there's about six rows of tables—like planks—running across it and down the sides. Everybody crowds in and when it's hot it stinks of food and frying."

"But Boyce liked it, so you all went?"

"Yeah," said Mobb. "Because the pies was good, too. And they was cheap."

"I see. What did you talk about?"

"In there? You couldn't get a word in edgeways."

"And you couldn't hear if you did," said Eric.

"Right. What next?"

128

"We went to the park, didn't we?"

"You're telling me, lad, not asking me."

"That's where we went."

"To do what? Sprawl on the grass?"

"Yes," said Eric. "There wasn't many people about. The office workers who'd been sitting on the benches eating sandwiches had gone back to work, and the mothers with kids weren't out yet. There were a few people with dogs, that's all."

"I can picture the scene," said Green. "With you three lying about on the grass, smoking fags and talking."

"That's right."

"So what was said? And tell me exactly, because that's when the real talking was done, wasn't it? When you were alone in the middle of a great playing field?"

Eric nodded glumly.

"Speak up, Eric," said his mother sharply.

He looked at her. "Norman said no bloody woman was going to treat him like that and get away with it."

"What woman was that?" asked Mrs Lawson.

"The woman magistrate," replied her son.

"Miss Foulger?" asked Green.

"That's her."

"What happened?"

"Ted asked him what he was going to do about it."

"You asked him, too," said Mobb.

"And what was his answer?"

"He said, 'We're gunna do'er, aren't we?' "

"Did he, now?"

"Yeah! He did."

"And what did you say?"

"We both told him he couldn't because the fuzz would know who'd done it straight away if he broke in there and smeared walls and things. He asked who was going to do that, and when we said he'd said he was, he said no, he'd simply said we'd do'er. And we would, but we were going to be very clever about it."

"What did he propose to do?"

Mobb replied. "Norm asked me if I ever watched telly and when

I said of course I did he said then I'd know how the fuzz works. They look at what they call the M.O. of every crime—he said that meant method of operating."

"It does—more or less."

"He said if we altered our M.O., you'd never get on to us. We wouldn't break anything or wreck the place and the fuzz would think it wasn't us."

"Why should they do that?" asked Green. "Seeing that as far as the police know you haven't committed any crime except the one you were up for last Tuesday, and on that occasion you didn't do any damage in the house, did you?"

"You dropped us right in it there," said Lawson to Mobb.

"I certainly think you tricked them," said Mrs Lawson.

"How, madam?"

"You got them to talk."

"Only to report on their conversation in the park. And be fair, I've just said that as far as the police know—and by that, I mean can prove—they are responsible for no other crimes."

"You mean you're not taking what has just been said as a confession?"

"I'm not taking any notes. Nor is anybody else. And what is more, love, I think you'll see the value of what this lad said just now. You see, there'll be no more crime from these two, because if there is, then what has just been said could be given in evidence. But as from now, these two are going to tread the straight and narrow. They've too much at stake to do anything else, and now Norman Boyce isn't here to suggest further break-ins . . ." Green didn't finish. He paused to let the warning sink in and for Mrs Lawson to appreciate that Mobb's words had put the two youths in a position from which there would be no escape in further crime.

After a long moment of silence, Mrs Lawson said: "I think you deserve that coffee now." She got to her feet. "I'll leave the kitchen door open so I can hear what goes on."

"You do that, love. We don't want to leave you out of anything. That's why we're here."

Green took out his battered cigarette packet. "Any of you jokers want a fag? Nobody? Good."

"You didn't give us a chance to answer," said Reed.

"You have to learn to be opportunist, Sergeant. Now, back to cases. Young Boyce said that you three had to alter your M.O. so that the police would be fooled into thinking that some other group had done your jobs. Did he say how he was going to change it?"

"Yes," replied Eric. "We weren't going to muck things up, but we were going to nick a few things."

"You'd never nicked anything before?"

"No."

"Why start now?"

"Norm said it was time we got ourselves a bit of bread. We needed more than the Social Security gave us."

Green turned to Sutcliffe. "Is it right they didn't steal anything?"

The constable nodded. "No reports of theft, sir. Just vandalism."

"Which is, if anything, worse than theft. Busting up everything people had worked for. Theft is greed, but vandalism is envy, and they're both deadly sins."

Mobb and Lawson looked abashed. Green said: "So what did Boyce say you were going to nick?"

"Mostly money if there was any. Then trannies and that sort of thing."

"Good," said Green. "But changing your M.O. wouldn't just mean nicking stuff instead of vandalising. You'd have had to change lots of things to fool the police. Like how you broke in, for instance."

Lawson looked at Mobb. "I told him that, didn't I?" He turned back to Green. "We'd never broken in. We'd only gone in where we found an open window."

"So?"

"I asked Norm how we were going to get in, seeing he'd said we'd have to change the methods. I told him that if we had to break windows there'd be a row to attract attention."

"And what had Boyce to say to that?"

"He said, 'Use your bonces, you two. I don't know how we're

going to get in—yet. We'll have to do what all the big boys do. We'll have to case it.'"

"It?"

"He meant we'd go along to Miss Foulger's house and look it over. He said we'd plan it and then keep our eyes open to see when she wasn't there. Then we'd get in by the way we reckoned best."

Mobb added: "He said we were going to make her pay for what she'd said. We'll give her idle good-for-nothings. We'll show her we're good enough to make *her* feel sorry for herself."

"That's right," said Lawson. "I pointed out to him that she wouldn't know it was us, but he said, maybe not, but she'd know it was somebody and that would make her think twice before running off at the mouth. In fact, he said we'd probably do her more than once. Let her get over the first time and then go in again. It'd cost her, he said."

"Did he say how?"

"He said all nobs like her had insurance and every time they got done the insurance cost more."

"He seems to have thought of everything."

"I know. I said I hadn't thought of that insurance business and he asked me if I ever thought of anything." He turned to face Mobb. "And you! You said all I could think about was my bird. 'Call me Coral, Eric, I like it better than Carol.'"

"To which, no doubt, your friend Boyce had a suitable reply?"

"He said it wasn't the only thing she liked . . ."

"Eric!" Mrs Lawson stood in the doorway with a tray of mugs of coffee.

"It's what he said, mum. And Ted here said, 'Hark who's talking. You and Pam Watson. What are you going to do about her, Norm? She's a cop's daughter.'"

"Oh yes," said Sutcliffe menacingly. "And what had your pal to say to that?"

"Nothing much. He said we'd go and look at Miss Foulger's house. It's out of town, a bit, and stands on its own. A sort of cottage."

"I know it," said Sutcliffe.

132

"What happened?" asked Green, acknowledging the receipt of a mug of coffee with a raised hand.

"Well, we went there, didn't we? If you go out of the park at the far corner—through the hedge—you come to the river . . ."

"River?" said Berger. "I didn't know Colesworth was on a river."

"Stream, Sarge," said Sutcliffe. "About four feet wide. Pretty though. It runs through a sort of shallow valley with a good few trees and bushes about."

"In other words, a good, covered approach route," said Green.

"For most of the way," admitted Lawson. "Then you have to go through a hedge into a big field where there was a herd of cows. We followed the hedge round . . ."

"Why? In case there was a bull there?"

"For cover," said Mobb. "We had to go round and then through the side hedge. That brought us out just near the end of the Foulger dame's garden."

"Go on."

"Well, we went in, didn't we? It's all fruit trees and currant bushes . . ."

"Plenty of cover, in fact."

"Yeah! And then we came to this little brick shed behind the house."

"The one Miss Foulger uses for wine making."

"We didn't know that then. It looked just like a little outhouse."

"So you broke in."

"No, we didn't. The door was open a bit."

"Are you trying to tell me anybody leaves an outhouse—with wine in it—unlocked, with people like you about?"

"It was open, honest," said Lawson. "It was an old green door, and it had a key in the lock. I remember that."

"I'll believe you—thousands wouldn't. So you went in. What happened?"

"Well . . . there was a row of bottles of wine on a sort of work bench under the window."

"And?"

"Norm grabbed the one nearest the door. He said he'd have it

133

because it was fullest. He was going to put it in the stream to cool it."

"Go on."

"I didn't want one. Ted didn't either."

"Don't like wine," said Mobb, "and it was too hot to carry a heavy bottle around."

"So what happened?"

"Norm got angry because we wouldn't take our bottles. He had his in his hand. He just stepped inside the shed and swept the others off the bench with the back of his other arm. He was really uptight about it."

"Go on."

"Well, it made a hell of a row, all those bottles breaking, so we scarpered."

"Back the way you came?"

"Down to the river. Norm put the bottle in the water for a bit then he took it out and started to drink the wine."

"How did he get the cork out?"

"Wasn't a cork. It was a white plastic thing. You could pull it out and put it back as often as you wanted."

Green glanced at Berger, who asked: "Did either of you have any of his wine?"

"He wouldn't give us any," said Mobb.

"You asked for some?"

"Well, it was bloody hot. I could have done with a swig. But he said we'd been too chicken to get bottles for ourselves so he wasn't going to share his."

"Lucky for you," said Berger. "Carry on with the story."

"Nothing else. It was getting on for tea-time, so we all came home."

"Each to his own home?"

"Where else?"

"But you met later? In the evening?"

"Ted and I met and went looking for Norm. He was still angry when we found him because his bird—Pam Watson, that is—hadn't turned up. We wandered about a bit, then Norm said he was very thirsty, like, and he was going into the pub for a drink."

134

"A pub where he was known?"

"Yeah! The Flag. We go there because they know we're over eighteen. Some of the other landlords won't serve us. Say we're not old enough."

Green privately thought that the said landlords were using lack of years as an excuse for not serving yobs, but he said nothing.

Berger continued the questioning.

"You went with him?"

"Yeah."

"How much did you have?"

"We had half each. Norm had two halves."

"When did you leave The Flag?"

"Just before closing time. Before half-ten."

"Was Boyce sober?"

"Well . . ."

"Was he?"

Lawson and Mobb looked at each other, both obviously disinclined to reply. Berger wasn't letting them off the hook, however. "Now listen to me, you two. You shot your mouths off to that reporter. You told him Boyce had only had two halves to drink. You didn't mention that he'd had a full bottle of probably very potent home-made wine before that. Why not?"

"Tell Mr Berger what he wants to know," said Mrs Lawson emphatically. "Go on, Eric, tell him."

"Don't bother," said Green. "We can guess. By the time you two got Boyce out of The Flag he was showing signs of being shot at, wasn't he? And you two bright Herberts, his pals, couldn't manage to get him home before he flaked out in front of Burton's, where Constable Sutcliffe found him. Right?"

"Yes," murmured Lawson.

"And you know what that means, don't you? It means that you hadn't enough nous to get help for him. If you had called for an ambulance, the hospital might have done something."

"How were we to know he'd been poisoned?"

"You weren't to know, lad, and that's the only thing you can congratulate yourselves on, because you hadn't the guts to stay with him when he crashed. You scarpered, leaving him alone to

135

be found by Constable Sutcliffe, who could only assume he was drunk. But why didn't you stay? I'll tell you why. You'd been let off only a few hours before with a strong warning not to get into trouble again, or else. And you thought that if you were caught with Boyce in that state, the fact that you'd been up to Miss Foulger's house with him would somehow leak out and you'd be nicked again, with every chance of being sent to Borstal."

Mobb, surprisingly, admitted the charge. "Only it wasn't quite like that," he said. "It was Norm who had pinched the wine; it was Norm who had broken the other bottles; it was Norm who had got drunk. We reckoned there was no sense in getting done for what we hadn't done. If we'd known he was ill—really sick instead of being just boozed-up, I mean—we'd have got him to the hospital. We would, straight up."

"That's right," added Lawson.

"Right. I'll believe you. But I've one last question to ask you."

"What's that?"

"Could Miss Foulger have got to know in any way whatsoever that you were going to visit her house?"

"No chance," said Mobb.

"You're sure you didn't talk about it in the Basement Café or the pie shop? That somebody didn't overhear you?"

"I'll swear to that," said Lawson. "Ted and I hadn't even thought about it until Norm told us in the park."

"Nobody heard you there?"

"Not a chance."

"Then how," asked Green quietly, "do you account for the fact that there was a nice bottle of poisoned wine all ready and waiting for you when you got there?"

Their two mouths fell open in surprise. "But that's . . . it's impossible," said Lawson.

"It happened, lad. Or are you going to tell me Miss Foulger was in the habit of leaving six bottles of poisoned wine in her outhouse on the offchance that somebody like you three would come along to nick it?"

"Six bottles?" asked Mobb.

"We'll never know for sure, will we, lad, because all the others were broken. Unless you're going to tell me that somehow, somebody knew exactly which bottle out of six your pal was going to pinch?"

"But that could mean that all three of us would have been dead by now," said Mobb.

"Right, lad. That's exactly what it could have meant. And that's one more good reason for not breaking into other people's homes in future and for not taking what doesn't belong to you."

"But she should be locked up."

"Who?"

"That Miss Foulger."

"Why?"

"Leaving poisoned wine about."

"On her own premises? Everybody in Colesworth who has a garden has something poisonous in the shed. I'll bet Mrs Lawson has something poisonous in her kitchen—bleach, cleaning fluid and the like. You want us to run them all in?"

"No, but . . ."

"The point is, lad, keep your hands off what doesn't belong to you. Then you can't come to any harm in the way your pal did."

"That's right," said Mrs Lawson firmly. "I only hope it's taught you two a lesson. As for you, Eric, you'll tell me in future exactly where you're going and what you're going to do. I'm going to keep an eye on you, my boy." She turned to Mobb, and for a moment, Green thought she was going to blast him. Instead, she said. "And the same applies to you. If you want to go about with Eric, you come here and tell me. Everything. And if you want girlfriends, they come here, too, so's I can see if they're suitable. And what I say goes in the future. Understood?"

Both youths, surprised out of their lives, nodded their agreement.

"Right. I know it will be a shock to your systems, but tomorrow I'm going to see about getting some work for you two to do. Even if it's only washing windows. I know a lot of people who haven't been able to get a window cleaner for years."

Green got to his feet. "We'll say goodnight, Mrs Lawson, and leave the three of you to your business meeting. Thanks for the coffee." He turned to the two boys. "There's a lot of money to be made as a window cleaner. And I mean by washing the glass, not by smashing it to help yourselves to other people's belongings. You behave yourselves, and Constable Sutcliffe here will recommend a few customers to you. You'll soon build up a round."

Chapter 7

IT WAS AFTER eleven o'clock when Green and Berger arrived at the Albatross Hotel. Masters and Reed were waiting for them.

"Time for a jar, if we're quick," said Masters. "I got the barman to hang on for a bit. Failing him, there's the night porter."

"Why not a cold one at the bar and a few bottles upstairs afterwards?"

"As you like. I take that to mean you've something to tell us."

"Only to report. Confirmation that the vino came from Foulger's. Boyce nicked it in the afternoon." They moved into the deserted bar where the lights were lowered and the barman was tidying up after a busy evening.

Masters ordered the beer. Green drank deep before saying: "What about Tom Watson? Did you sort them out?"

"I think I acted as catalyst. They only needed to be brought together and made to talk. The girl herself had the answer. She's decided to have an abortion. Mrs W didn't like the idea at bottom, but she accepted it as the best solution to a problem which could ruin all their lives."

"How did Tom take it?"

"After he got over thinking I'd gone there to put his girl through the hoop, with a strong possibility of arresting her for murder, he accepted the outcome with a noticeable sense of relief. You could actually feel a lot of the misery and mistrust lift out of all of them."

"So you're pleased you went."

"Very pleased."

"Even though old Tom Watson was all set to plant one on him," said Reed.

Green stared. "He what?"

"He squared up to the Chief. I got in between them quick."

"Good for you, lad. If Watson had taken a swing at His Nibs . . . well, striking a superior officer isn't viewed very favourably. Tom Watson would have been out on his ear tomorrow."

"I was afraid he'd have been out on the floor tonight. Flat out. If the Chief had retaliated he'd have made mincemeat of Watson. Don't you remember that chap he hit near Paddington? I thought we'd never get him round and he was a big strong bloke."

Green grinned. "I actually saw that punch," he said with great pleasure. "I'd have liked a movie shot of it. Funny, really, though, because His Nibs doesn't like using his mitts. Frightened of getting them dirty on a villain's hide, I suppose."

Masters, who had missed most of this conversation because of a few words with Berger, turned back to Green. "Yes, I was pleased I visited the Watsons', but for one awful moment I thought Tom would go for me. I was wondering how I'd be able to keep it quiet if he did. I wouldn't have wanted to spoil his career just because I'd taken it into my head to do a bit of do-gooding."

"Most do-gooders ruin more lives than enough."

"Meaning I ought not to have gone?"

"Meaning I shouldn't have let you, I should have gone instead."

Masters put down his empty tankard. "Maybe. Now, what about going up? Reed, tell the night porter I'd like eight cold bottles sent up."

"Right, Chief."

Green, whose memory was renowned for its accuracy, had almost finished his account of his evening's work when the phone in the bedroom rang. Masters answered it. It was Professor Haywood.

"Haven't disturbed your beauty sleep have I, old boy? No? Good, because you've had me working ever since I left you at teatime."

"Sorry to hear that, Professor."

"Sorry, nothing. Your brainwave paid off. At least I hope you think it did."

"Do I take it you found something interesting on Boyce's boots?"

"In the soles. They're rubber, you know. Thick rubber with a very pronounced and deep cut pattern."

"Deep enough to hold a bit of evidence for about ten hours, you think?"

"Ten hours? Ten days probably. Tiny pieces of glass embedded . . ."

"Ah!"

"Don't tell me. That is exactly what you were expecting."

"Not expecting exactly. Hoping for would be nearer the mark. And, of course, the type of glass—or types—is going to make a difference."

"Which are you hoping for most?"

"Well, now, as I now know he broke five bottles of white wine, I would expect to find some white or pale green bottle glass. That is unless Miss Foulger put her wine into brown bottles. Somehow, I don't think she would. However, that is beside the point. But were you to find shards of actinic glass . . ."

"Now it's my turn to say, 'Ah!'?"

"Meaning what exactly?"

"A tiny sliver of pure brown actinic glass, and quite a large piece—over a quarter of an inch long—with the remains of the greyish ceramic collar one finds on capsules."

"So that piece is part of a neck?"

"Yes. It's concave with a narrow diameter. It was lodged in one of the treads of the pattern."

"Thank you, Professor."

"I suppose it tells you a lot."

"It certainly tells me that the wine was doctored where Boyce found it, unless we intend to consider a coincidence so great that I doubt whether any computer ever built could calculate the chances."

"How come?"

"I mean that Boyce should pick up an actinic glass shard from a capsule on the day on which he was killed by the contents of just such a container in some place other than the one where he found the wine."

"I think I get that. I think you'd be right to ignore it, otherwise your investigations would become as convoluted as your explanations."

"Thanks."

"It's a pleasure. Now, as I've been working all night while you people have been living it up . . ."

"Correction, Professor. We are all four just home after a full night's work."

"Really?"

"The truth, Professor. We were just exchanging results when you rang. We are all four here in my room."

"You wouldn't have a cold drink there, would you?"

"As a matter of fact, we have. Are you coming to join us?"

"Expect me in ten minutes."

"Right." Masters put down the phone. "Berger, please ask the night porter for another half dozen bottles of iced beer and tell him to expect Professor Haywood."

"Right, Chief."

Green glugged another beer into his tankard and said: "So we've got to look at La Foulger, have we?"

"I should hope so," said Berger. "Hers the wine and hers the poison."

"And hers the premises," added Masters. "You got the gist of Haywood's call, I suppose?"

"Every word," said Green. "Both going and coming. Funny how some phones act like loud-speakers, while some won't ackle at all."

"Ackle or crackle?" asked Berger.

"They all crackle or whine," grunted Green.

"Time's own Garments," murmured Masters.

"You what?"

"Sorry. I was maundering. When you spoke about the noise a phone makes."

"Time's own Garments? Where's the . . . er . . . connection?"

"Not poetry at this time of night, Chief," pleaded Berger.

"The trouble with the young," said Green, "and among them I include you, Sergeant Berger, as well as sundry others like Lawson and Mobb, is that you have no soul and no culture. I've loved poetry all my life. I started learning verse when I was three, hence my encyclopaedic knowledge of the subject."

"You didn't know the bit the Chief just quoted."

"No . . . o."

"And I bet you can't remember the first verse you ever learned."

"I can, you know."

"Let's hear it, then."

"I thought you said you didn't want to hear any poetry. But since you've changed your mind . . ." Green changed his voice to falsetto, and quoted, childlike:

> "One, two, three, my mother caught a flea.
> She put it in the teapot to make a cup of tea.
> The flea jumped out and made mother shout . . ."

At that point the door opened and Haywood said:

> "Here comes father with his tongue hanging out."

Green gazed at him in surprise. "You know that one, do you Prof?"

"Sure. It's one of the old skipping rhymes. The pitch, patch, pepper group." He joined Green in the middle of the floor. Together they recited:

> "Oliver Cromwell lost his shoe,
> At the battle of Waterloo,
> Pitch, patch, pepper."

"Cut it out for heaven's sake," said Masters. "All the other guests will be complaining."

"You started it," accused Green. "Time's own Garments!"

Masters said: "Beer for the Professor, please Reed. He's had a long, hard day."

The beer was cold enough to frost the pressed glass of the tankard. Haywood took it gratefully and lifted it. "Here's to the good of your health," he said.

"Here's to the health of your blood," answered Green.

Together they intoned:

"You can't have good health without good blood,
So here's to your bloody good health."

"They're both kalied," said Berger. "It must be the heat or something they ate."

"The show's over," said Masters. "Sit down, please, everybody."

As they settled he turned to Haywood. "I've got a problem."

"I'm sure."

"Bill Green learned tonight from one of our dead friend's pals that Boyce nicked one of a row of bottles of wine and then smartly broke all the rest."

Haywood nodded to show he'd got the picture.

"The youth said that Boyce chose the fullest bottle. The one with most wine in it. So I presume he meant that the liquid was furthest up the neck."

"That follows. It was the one that had had the gold solution added to it."

"Quite. But you told us there were two thousand milligrams of gold salt in the bottle."

"That's right. Checked and rechecked."

"You also said that the ampoules—of all strengths, hold one mil."

"Right again."

"If the strongest dosage is fifty milligrams in one mil . . ."

"It is."

"It would take forty mils of liquid to hold it."

"Right again."

"Or eight good teaspoons of liquid."

"Yes."

"That's too much to go on top of an already full bottle of wine."

"Levels in full bottles differ, you know, but I see what you mean. Forty mils is nearly one and a half fluid ounces. Over one and a third, anyway."

"Couldn't whoever put it in have poured some of the wine away, Chief?" asked Reed.

"I suppose he could have done," agreed Masters, "but I don't visualise it like that. I could be all wrong."

"No, you're not," said Green surprisingly. "Our chap whipped the cork out and started emptying his poison in. He wasn't thinking of levels or overflowing or anything like that. If he'd had too much for one bottle he'd have gone on to the next."

"We don't know he didn't," said Reed.

"We do, lad. The two thousand milligrams the Prof has told us were in the bottle make a good round figure. A big, good round figure. I reckon we can go nap on him not having more than that or him not having two thousand one hundred and ten or some such figure."

"I agree with that," said Haywood. "That two thousand is a very accurate figure. If your man had doctored more bottles, there wouldn't have been two thousand exactly in Boyce's drink. Besides, I cannot really believe anybody could get away with that much aurothiomalate, let alone more." He turned to Masters. "It seems like a bit of a poser for you, but there's nothing I can suggest that will help."

"We'll manage," said Green. "Now, what about another forty— or four hundred—mils of beer, Prof?"

"Thank you. The latter figure would be the more to my liking."

As Masters reached the breakfast table, he said to Green who was already there, alone, and eating: "No potato this morning?"

"Fried bread instead," said Green through a crunching mouthful. "I reckon word got round among the chefs that after our chat in the kitchen yesterday we were not to be given any favours. So they sent word back that they had no spud to fry for me. So I sent the waiter back for fried bread. They couldn't say they hadn't any bread, could they?"

"Hardly. But they're not acting the fool are they? They're not denying us anything else?"

"No . . . o," said Green. "But what extra I've asked for—like a couple of sausages to go with my egg and bacon—is going to be added to the bill."

"They said so?"

"I could see it on the waiter's face. We'll have to wrap this one up quick, George, otherwise we shall find ourselves . . . what's that latin saying? . . . persons au gratin?"

"That's more or less right. At any rate I grasp the meaning." Masters broke off to give the waiter his order for orange juice and scrambled eggs and then went on: "Oh, by the way, Bill, I want to thank you for backing me up last night over the business of the amount of fluid in the bottle. I'm afraid the others didn't quite see it my way. You obviously did."

"Think nothing of it," said Green stretching for more toast. "I could visualise what you were getting at and it seemed natural to me. Even if I hadn't seen it the same way, you had a fifty per cent chance of being right, so it was a good enough bet."

"Thanks all the same."

Green put his knife and fork down. "George, I've known you long enough to recognise certain signs. When you go all absent minded and start quoting bits about the garments of time, I know you're not really with us. Your old brain has seen a way through the ice floes and you're starting to head for open water. If you suddenly shouted, 'There she blows!' at such a time I'd pay attention because I reckon it would have some meaning. So when you start asking about the volume of poison in a bottle I realise it will—most likely—have some relevance. That's it. End of explanation." He took up his knife and fork again. "Now I'd better finish this before it gets cold. I don't like congealed eggs."

The two sergeants came down together.

"You're late," growled Green.

"After that schemozzle last night, I'm surprised we're here at all."

"Cut the lip and look slippy," ordered Green. "We've got a lot to do."

"Like what?"

Green was stumped for specifics, not having discussed the programme with Masters, but he wasn't for being beaten.

"You two," he said, "have to comb this town to find that bottle. After that you can print it, then go to the morgue and take Boyce's dabs. Compare the two. After lunch you can empty Miss Foulger's dustbin. We want all the broken glass sifted out and then separated."

Reed asked: "He's not serious, is he, Chief?"

"Why not? I think it would be a good idea to phone Miss Foulger, because a lot of these home wine-makers use their own labels, so it will help you to identify what you are looking for—if she had already labelled those particular bottles. If not . . . well, I don't suppose Boyce finished his wine before he got home. So the bottle could be there. But ask the other two tearaways if he did finish it and sling it somewhere. If that happened you should be able to pick it up."

Berger looked at Reed. "In this heat!" he said.

"And I shall want the car," added Masters.

Reed said: "I don't think I really want any breakfast."

"Get the murder bag out of the boot," said Green. "You'll want that for dusting and photographing. Best carry it with you, then you won't have to walk to and fro each time you want to use it."

Green took out his cigarettes. "More coffee, George?" he asked. "Or another plate of gammon, perhaps?"

Masters grinned. "I think we've had enough of both." He looked across at the two glum sergeants. "Get down in time, in future," he said. "I want to be away in five minutes flat." He pushed back his chair and got to his feet.

"You mean all that about looking for the bottle was all eyewash, Chief?"

"Not eyewash. A warning and an unofficial reprimand. Hurry it up."

As Masters stood at the open door of the hotel filling his first pipe of the day, Green joined him.

"Bill, do I remember young Sutcliffe said he visited a chemist on Tuesday?"

"That's right. But . . ."

"But what?"

"You're not thinking that the lad somehow got hold of the stuff when he went there?"

"No, no. I just want to talk to a retail pharmacist. A practical chap. Haywood is fine as a forensic buff, but I feel the need to get down out of his clouds on to the good earth."

"I never thought the day would come when I would hear you say that, George."

Masters applied the match to his pipe. "Why not?"

"Because you usually revel in the academic side of investigation."

"Agreed. But what do I do when I feel that the top brass on the academic side has not given us everything I feel he should?"

"Are you saying Haywood has misled us?"

"Not deliberately. My opinion of the man is that he would never do that. In fact, I trust his integrity."

"What then?"

"Some fact, which he as a clever man in his field knows so well that he thinks everybody must know it."

"I'm with you. Like the boffins in the botulism case. They said that type E was found only in the northern hemisphere and spread pretty thinly on the ground. By that they meant it was in the sea, too, but we took them literally, at first."

"That's it, Bill. There's some fact like that which we haven't got hold of yet."

Green shaded his eyes against the morning sun and took his time before asking the obvious question. "What makes you so sure, George?"

Masters was equally slow in replying, as though thinking out how best to word his reply in the most convincing way.

"Last night it was suggested that our murderer emptied some of the wine from the bottle. I don't think he did, for all sorts of reasons like how difficult it is to judge how much to pour away, how much he is going to add and so on. But I will concede that it is a palpably weak point in my argument, because I have no proof and it is based purely on a gut feeling."

"None the worse for that at this stage. I agreed with you, remember."

"Which was good to hear, but which nevertheless adds no more proof to the conviction."

"So last night you stayed awake for hours thinking it over."

"For a few minutes, certainly."

"And you came up with even more gut feelings—probably more convincing this time."

"Right. To get two thousand milligrams of the gold solution into that bottle, and using the strongest preparation—fifty milligrams in a one mil tube—our man would have to stand in that shed and open forty glass ampoules and empty them very carefully into the bottle."

"Meaning he must have exercised extreme care otherwise he wouldn't have got all two thousand milligrams in?"

"That's it. He would have to take time to drain and shake each one, wiping the edge on the neck of the bottle to get the last drop out. How long would snapping open and emptying forty capsules in that way take?"

"Dunno, exactly. But if the chap doing them was not used to the job—well, say at least a minute each, bearing in mind he would have to take them, presumably, from their box and put them back again as well as all the other taradiddle; I'm assuming he wouldn't drop the ampoules on the floor, only the snapped off tops. Boyce picked one of those up in the sole of his boot, but he didn't pick up much more, whereas he would have done had there been forty ampoules sculling about the deck."

"So the man stayed there a minimum of forty minutes by your reckoning?"

"A minimum of forty. If they only took ten seconds a tube longer it would mean a further six or seven minutes."

"So what's the answer, Bill? Would a poisoner risk hanging about on the job for three quarters of an hour?"

"Definitely not—in my opinion. I think that is the strongest argument you've come up with to support your views, George. But Haywood can't be expected to consider how long a criminal spends on his task."

"He can't," admitted Masters, "and so he must be overlooking something. He must be."

"So we go to see your chemist first?"

Masters shook his head. "I rang the station earlier. The court sits today at half past ten and Miss Foulger is presiding. I want to see her today, so I've got to get there before she leaves to take up the sword of justice . . . ah, here they are."

The two sergeants joined them.

"Right. To the station first to pick up Betty Prior, and let's be quick about it."

With the W.P.C. as guide, they reached Miss Foulger's cottage a few minutes after nine o'clock. The magistrate, dressed in flowered overall and headscarf, was dusting the hall when Masters reached the open front door.

"Good morning, ma'am. Am I speaking to Miss Foulger?"

"You are."

"Then I'd better identify myself. I am Detective Chief Superintendent Masters of Scotland Yard . . ."

"Have you your card?"

Masters rarely showed his warrant, but he did so now. After taking it with rheumaticky fingers and scrutinising it closely and inspecting his features, she handed it back.

"Can't be too careful with strangers, you know."

"Quite right, ma'am. I have with me three colleagues from the Yard and W.P.C. Prior from the local force who is acting as our guide."

"Know her," said Miss Foulger, giving Betty a nod of recognition. "These others . . . ?"

Masters introduced them individually.

"What can I do for you? Want a search warrant signed?"

"No, ma'am. We have come to talk to you about the murder of the youth, Boyce."

"Idle young layabout. Had him in front of us last Tuesday. Let him go, of course."

"A pity, as it turned out, ma'am," said Green. "If you'd given him a custodial sentence he might still be alive."

"Suppose so. But we're not clairvoyant on the bench, you know."

"That, too, is a pity," said Masters.

"What do you mean? Criticising our sentences, are you? If so, I need hardly tell you . . ."

"Not your sentences," cut in Masters.

"What then?"

"Your homilies from the bench, ma'am. It was what you had to say to young Boyce and his friends—or the way you said it—that drove him to the decision to break into your home."

"Nobody has broken into my home."

"Into your property. He smashed your bottles of wine."

"Did he, indeed!"

"But he kept one back to drink."

"Theft as well as vandalism, eh?"

"And murder, ma'am. He died that night as a direct result of drinking that bottle of wine from your store shed."

"Nonsense. That was good, fine wine."

"You would have a hard time convincing Professor Haywood of that, ma'am. All his tests show the wine to have contained a large amount of toxic substance."

"Impossible."

"Now ma'am," said Masters, "as a magistrate you will appreciate that we have to get to the bottom of this apparent paradox. So could we step inside and discuss it thoroughly and exhaustively?"

"I am due in court . . ."

"At half past ten, ma'am, I know. I shall make sure my car gets you there in good time, but the sooner we get started, the more comfortable the time margin will be."

She led them in, through the highly polished hall, small and scarcely roomy enough for so great a number of big men, into a garden sitting room. This too was small, but had a number of chairs, no two alike, but all covered in bottle green velvet. The french window gave on to the garden which boasted no well-kept symmetry, but rather a comfortable and shaggy nonchalance: a garden tended for colour and what it would produce rather than for prize-winning lay out.

"The old laundry is out here," she said, moving to the open half of the french window. "Over to the right there. It is nearer or more available to the back door than to this one. Its door is on the far end."

Masters peered out and then turned to her.

"You bottle your wine out there?"

"Because it is an old laundry, really, and so has water and a sink for cleaning bottles and utensils. After bottling, I transfer my wines to the small cellar I have below the front of the cottage."

"And where does it ferment, or whatever the term is?"

"Under the stairway. You see, all the areas I can use for my hobby are quite tiny, so I have to have a different workshop, as it were, for each part of the process."

"So can we talk about the wine which young Boyce stole from you?"

"It was not poisoned, Mr Masters."

"Not by you, perhaps, ma'am. But I assure you it killed the lad."

"I don't understand it at all." She sat down and the rest followed suit. "Nothing of this sort has ever happened to my wine before, and I would swear that particular racking was as sweet and wholesome as could be."

"What sort of wine was it?" asked Green.

"Rose petal."

"Rose . . . petal?"

"Yes. White and yellow petals—no leaves or stalk. That makes the wine bitter. But for a white wine—pale golden, actually, use the pale petals. Dark red petals give a red wine, of course."

"But isn't it perfumed?" asked Green. "Sort of bath essencey?"

"Delicately scented, dependent upon how pungent the flowers are. I pick them when full blown. But the point about rose petal wine is that you can make it throughout the summer months because the flowering season is so long and prolific. And, of course, it only takes about a month from picking the flowers to bottling."

"How do you start?" asked Green. "By boiling the flowers and adding sugar?"

"No, no, no. That is absolutely fatal. You must not boil the flowers or pour boiling water over them. You wash them, of course, in case a bird or pest spray has fouled them."

"I see."

"For flower wines, one must prepare the must first, and then . . ."

"Must?" asked Reed. "That sounds as if it had gone mouldy."

"The name we give to grape juice or sugar solution which forms

152

the basis of wine fermentation. You're thinking of mustiness."

"Sorry ma'am."

"For rose petal wine I use a white grape concentrate with as little taste as possible, and I add about one pound of sugar to the gallon of must. And as a starter—that is the agent to start fermentation—I use a good white-wine yeast."

"Ah, yes, of course. Yeast."

"I leave this for a few days to let the first violent fermentation die down before adding the petals. The reason for this is obvious."

"Oh, is it?" asked Green. "Not to me it isn't."

"During fermentation, carbon dioxide is bubbled off. This would carry away the volatile esters and essential oils that give the petals their fragrance and flavour. So I wait until the vigorous activity in the fermentation vessel is over. Then I add my petals in a muslin bag. By that time there is enough alcohol in the must to draw out the scent, colour and flavour. And I assure you that nothing unwholesome got into the vessel. Every petal was hand picked and washed by me, and the vessel itself had a snap seal lid with a fermentation lock firmly fixed in a rubber grummet. The only times the vessel was opened was once daily when I had to squeeze the bag of petals with a plastic spoon. After five days I transferred the must to the fermentation jar—with a lock, of course."

"For four weeks, you said?"

"That's right. Then I bottled it last Tuesday morning."

"Why then? When you were due in court at half past ten?"

"Because," said Miss Foulger patiently, "the final step before you bottle rose wine is the addition of a crushed Campden tablet."

"What's that?" asked Green suspiciously.

"Sodium metabisulphite. It gives sulphur dioxide. It's used in lots of food."

"It's all right," said Masters. "Campden tablets are quite harmless." He turned to Miss Foulger. "What is their purpose in the process?"

"As a stabiliser and anti-oxidant. It helps the wine keep."

"But why is timing so critical?"

"Because while the wine is in the jar, it settles and clears. When

153

it is clear and bright, you have to add the Campden tablet to keep it stable in that condition."

"When did you add the tablet?"

"On Monday morning. That was when it was best to add it. And you have to bottle the wine twenty-four hours after adding the tablet. Not that it is vital to a few minutes, but I was going to be away all day in court and out in the evening, so I had to do it before I set off."

"No choice but Tuesday morning then," said Green glumly.

"None whatever."

"What sort of bottles did you use?" asked Masters.

"Bordeaux bottles."

"What are they?" asked Reed.

"Square shouldered, clear glass, of course."

"Oh, yes, of course."

"Punted."

"I . . . er . . . beg your pardon?"

"Punted," said Masters, "means they have an indented base."

"Oh, that, Chief!"

That settled, Miss Foulger pressed on. "The important thing, once the wine is bottled, is to get it stoppered, to prevent wild yeasts getting in and ruining it. I had sterilised my stoppers ready for insertion. I use the white polythene flanged type, chiefly because I have arthritis and they are easier for me to handle than corks and lever-actioned corkers or corking guns. There are other advantages with polythene stoppers of course. The first being that they are easily sterilised and they are also reusable. The second is that they don't have to be kept damp like a cork, and so one can stand the bottles upright, which is better for me on my particular shelving."

"And that is how you left your bottles?"

"Yes. There were six of them. Each bottle holds just over twenty-six fluid ounces, you see, so a gallon just nicely fills six. I had intended on Wednesday morning to cover the stoppers with viscose capsules. You know what they are—the skirts that cover the tops of the necks and closures. One applies them wet, and they shrink to a tight fit."

"Why wait to do it?" asked Green.

"Because I had no time on Tuesday morning, and also because another advantage of the polythene stopper is that it will blow without the bottle bursting should the wine, by any mischance, start to ferment again. It is, therefore, advisable to wait for a day or so before putting on the viscose. Just to make sure there is no movement starting up again."

Masters leaned forward. "One last question on this particular point, Miss Foulger. How full were the bottles?"

"How full? I always try to level them out to about an inch below where the bottom of a cork would come. And this is what I did on Tuesday. But you must realise that polythene stoppers are hollow, and so it is possible to fill to much nearer the top of the neck should you have the wine to do so."

Masters looked across at Green, who stared back.

"Now the shed, Miss Foulger. Did you leave it open or locked?"

"Definitely locked."

"So somebody had to break in to get at the wine."

"No. When I arrived home on Tuesday evening, I found the key in the door. You see, Chief Superintendent, I do what you will say is a foolish thing. I hide that key on the ledge above the door . . ."

Green grunted in disgust.

". . . and I suppose somebody came and discovered it."

"Or knew where to look for it," said Green. "Somebody who knew he could tamper with your wine because he knew your habits and where you always left that key."

"I never imagined . . ."

"Miss Foulger," said Masters. "I imagine you have been a J.P. for a good many years. Surely the stories you have heard in the magistrates' court should have alerted you to the fact that these days there are those who will break in anywhere for little or no reason?"

"I should have known better," she confessed.

"Now ma'am," said Masters, "positively the last question. Have you ever had gold injections for your arthritis?"

"What an extraordinary question to ask in the middle of a murder investigation."

"Have you?"

"Never. And I'm pleased I haven't. Some of my acquaint-ances—I belong to the Arthritis and Rheumatism Club, you know—have had gold injections. They can be quite painful in themselves, I'm told."

"So there will be no gold injection ampoules anywhere in the house or the shed."

"No. I have my tablets—the same ones I've been on for years."

"Thank you. And now ma'am, if we're to get you to the court on time . . ."

Miss Foulger stood up. "I shall be ready in five minutes, Mr Masters."

After they had deposited Miss Foulger, once more resplendent in her costume—despite the persistent heat—Betty Prior directed Reed, who was driving, to the chemist's shop in Park Street which Sutcliffe had visited on Tuesday morning on his way home after the court hearing.

"Stay with the car, you three. The D.C.I. will come with me. We don't want to swamp the shop."

Green and Masters entered the shop in silence.

"I would like to speak to the pharmacist, please. My name is Masters and I'm a police officer from Scotland Yard."

The woman behind the counter looked a little taken aback, but she answered straight away. "I'll tell my husband you are here."

From the dispensary behind the counter came the clack of a typewriter being used inexpertly. It stopped a second or two after the woman had left the counter.

"His name's Morton," said Green. "It's on his notice. A. R. Morton, F.P.S."

A middle-aged, white-coated man appeared closely followed by the woman.

"I am the pharmacist. My name is Morton."

"This is D.C.I. Green and my name is Masters."

"Ah! The chaps who are looking into the mysterious death at the police station. I'd heard you were here. What can I do for you?"

"Give us the benefit of your advice and knowledge I hope, Mr

Morton. Is there somewhere where we can speak privately?"

"Will the dispensary do?"

"Capital."

"Come round the counter, then. I must say it is a relief to hear you only want my advice and that you haven't come to question me about something I've dispensed. I think most chemists would begin to feel a bit uneasy if they were told Masters of the Yard was in their shop asking for them."

By this time they were all in the dispensary where Morton had been making up scripts and typing the labels. "There'll be a rush in a minute or two. People coming back to collect their medicines."

"Business slack, is it?" asked Green.

"Not as brisk as it might be. The supermarkets sell so many of our lines these days. Chemists are going out of business every day. But you're not here to discuss the state of my business, I take it?"

"No," admitted Masters, "and to be quite honest with you, I don't know exactly what I am after. If I did, I probably wouldn't be here."

Morton seemed to catch on. "The lad died in the cell, I believe?"

"Yes."

"Violence on the part of the police?"

"None."

"By anybody?"

"No. The body was unmarked."

"Too young for a heart attack, one would suppose. So, if he was not previously suffering from some fatal disease, I must assume he was poisoned and that's why you're here. Something about some toxic substance, perhaps?"

"You've guessed it, mate," said Green.

"But surely you have a pathologist who can tell you what killed him?"

"Oh, yes. Professor Haywood."

"He's a known man in the forensic field. I don't think I could tell you anything he couldn't."

Masters glanced round at the racks of dispensing containers, all varying in size and the amounts of their contents still remaining.

"I think possibly you can, because you are a practical man."

"Ah! Haywood is academically and theoretically excellent, but . . . is that it?"

"That is my feeling. You will know soon enough, Mr Morton, that young Boyce was killed by a massive dose of sodium aurothiomalate."

"Gold? Poisoned by gold?"

"You didn't know it could be dangerous stuff?"

"Of course I knew. I handle it frequently. Not every day of course because it is now a comparatively rare treatment, but arthritis is still the biggest disease in the country, so even if only a small percentage use gold salts, it is still noticeable."

"I'm sorry. I shouldn't have asked that question. It sounded as though I doubted your professional knowledge."

"Nonsense. It was purely rhetorical. But to get back to the lad who died. You said he had a massive dose. How much? A hundred and fifty or two hundred milligrams?"

"Two hundred?" said Green scornfully. "Two thousand."

"Two thousand! You're joking."

"I assure you we're not, Mr Morton. Professor Haywood has discovered exactly that amount in the body."

"By extrapolation or however it is these forensic boys do their calculations?"

"Quite."

"Well I don't think I'd try to argue with Haywood over his figures. But two thousand! At first, you see, I thought you were going to say the boy was sensitive to the stuff. In that case a couple of hundred milligrams would be very, very dangerous. But with two thousand—well you don't have to be sensitive to it to keel over with that amount. Why, it's forty times the current maximum dose."

"So," said Masters, "where did it come from?"

"Not from me, at any rate," said Morton decisively. "I've never carried that amount. I buy ten ampoules at a time, simply because that is how the manufacturer puts them up. If he sold them in half-dozens, I'd buy them six at a time."

"You know what the next question is going to be, don't you, Mr Morton?"

"Yes. Who would carry such an amount? And the answer is, the manufacturer, a pharmaceutical wholesaler, or a central hospital pharmacy."

"Central pharmacy?"

"Yes. Hospitals tend to buy drugs in administrative groupings these days to get better contract prices. The Group Chief Pharmacist then presides over a central dispensary to which is attached the group store—usually at the biggest general hospital in the area. A G.C.P. would have two thousand milligrams of sodium aurothiomalate alongside him because it is more widely used by hospital rheumatologists than by G.P.s."

"I see. Thank you. So you never have more than five hundred milligrams on the premises?"

"Let me see, now. I don't buy the fifty milligram ampoules."

"Never?"

"No. I make the necessary amounts up by multiples of twenty milligram and ten milligram ampoules. I can dispense any amount by having six ampoules each of the one, five, ten and twenty strengths. That works out at a total of . . . six, plus thirty, plus . . . two hundred and sixteen milligrams, but as I re-order before I'm completely out of stock, call it three hundred as a maximum."

"I see. That is all very clear. Do all pharmacists shun the fifty milligram ampoules?"

"Quite a lot do. But if you have only a couple of local patients on fifty a month each, it would be worthwhile stocking that strength."

"So your profession has not refused to stock the fifty milligram ampoules to the stage where the manufacturers have been obliged to stop making it?"

"Lord, no. Not like the old two hundred milligram strength."

Masters said very slowly: "Please say that again."

Morton stared at him. "The two hundred milligram . . . No, no, Chief Superintendent. It won't work. Those ampoules were stopped more than ten years ago."

"Tell us," invited Green heavily.

"Well," said Morton, scratching one ear as an aid to thought, "when gold treatment first came in, it was tried on patients in whom all other previous treatments had failed, and it did the trick.

Highly successful in a number of cases, in fact. And all the indications were that success was dose-related . . ."

"Does that mean that the bigger the dose, the more relief could be expected?" asked Masters.

"That's it. And this was true, but like most treatments, though it gave more relief from arthritis, it began to create its own side-effects and these meant that limited doses only should be used. But before the side-effects became apparent—because, as I remember they were not immediate . . ."

"Insidious?"

"Not quite. As I remember it—and don't forget I'm not a pharmacologist, so my memory may be faulty—in most cases the undesirable effects became apparent when total dosage reached a certain figure. What I mean is, and I'm trying to remember the cases, certain patients were given fifty milligrams at weekly and then monthly intervals and they got great relief until the total dosage reached eight hundred or a thousand or some such figure. Then, side-effects were detected. So they had to come off the treatment. But this sort of effect can only be detected after prolonged use. And until it was detected and the warnings went out, there was a two hundred milligram ampoule for seriously crippled patients."

"Who had all got side effects by the time it was stopped," grunted Green.

"Not at all. Gold has no ill-effects at all on some people. But because there are some who have or who develop a sensitivity to it, the medical profession has to go very cautiously with everybody, testing for side-effects at frequent intervals."

"I think we've understood that, Mr Morton. The big ampoules went off the market more than ten years ago, you say?"

"At least that. But they weren't bigger ampoules. They still held one mil, just as the present ones of all strengths do. The contents were just more highly concentrated."

Masters nodded to show he understood. "So nobody can now get hold of the two hundred strength?"

"No. Certainly no pharmacist would have them, because like foodstuffs, medicines have a restricted shelf life. Three years is the overall average. We return out-of-date stocks to the manufacturers."

"Are you saying that after three years the gold salt would be useless?"

"No. What I am saying is that it is illegal to use any drug, after the end of its registered shelf life, for dispensing to humans. For that reason, no pharmacist would keep such stocks."

Mrs Morton put her head round the door.

"It's Mrs Rhodes, Arthur. Is her medicine ready?"

"Oh, dear. No . . ." He turned to Masters. "You will have to excuse me."

"Of course. We'll go. Thank you very much for giving us so much of your time, Mr Morton."

"I hope I've helped you, but it seems I've probably complicated matters for you."

"Not at all. Goodbye and thank you once again."

As they left the shop, Green said: "There you are. I always said you were a jammy bastard, George."

Masters laughed. "Jammy? Because I felt it in my bones that Haywood's report was not complete? Come on, Bill, you're the one who has always told the rest of us not to rely solely on experts. I heard you saying as much to Wanda a couple of weeks ago."

"Giving her the benefit, was I?"

"Benefit? You were slandering her butcher if I remember rightly."

"Putting the girlie in the picture," said Green, who always gave the impression that Wanda Masters and her infant son, Michael William, were the reasons for the world's creation and his own continued existence therein. "I pointed out to her that the expert butcher in whom she had every confidence was just the clever sort of artist who could con her. As he had done. She'd asked for a joint of topside for roasting. Next to the topside is the silverside and that's not for roasting, it's for pickling."

"Putting down in salt, you mean?"

"Exactly. And Wanda's expert butcher had cut across the dividing line and charged her top whack for a mish-mash of a joint that was neither one thing nor the other. He got away with it because Wanda knows he is a properly trained master-butcher. If it had been his shop boy who cut that joint for her she'd have noticed there was something wrong. Dammit, George, the grain of the meat changed direction in the middle. I'd like to bet when you carved that joint you wondered what the hell, because one moment you'd have been cutting properly, across the fibres, and the next you'd have been cutting with them and lobbing up slabs of string."

"I remember that. I did wonder about it."

"There you are then. And talking of meat . . ."

"Yes?"

"There's the car and the other three. Shall we try and get a cup of coffee? It's gone eleven o'clock, and I'm clammed."

"It's all the talking you do." Masters went to the car. "I take it you've improved the shining hour and had coffee?"

"No, Chief."

"Come on, then. Betty, where's the nearest place?"

"It's an oldy tea shoppy just round the corner, Chief."

"Lead on. The D.C.I. is wilting from thirst."

The little café stood a few feet back beyond a cobbled apron. It had a gaily striped awning to welcome customers, and a very large Alsatian to deter those who didn't propose to behave. It rose and casually sniffed at Green as he entered.

"Keep that thing at bay," he said. "I know it's as gentle as a lamb, but it still makes me nervous."

"Down, Chopper," said the girl who came forward to indicate a table and to take their order.

"Chopper?" said Green in dismay.

"Short for helicopter," said the girl. "We could hardly call him Helly, could we?"

Green didn't reply. He decided he'd have a home-made rock cake with his coffee and turned to Masters. "We were talking about beef."

"You mean it has some relevance—other than the tuition you gave to Wanda about buying her Sunday joint?"

"I do," said Green, missing the opportunity to point out that it was Masters who had brought up the subject in the first place. "In the army . . ."

162

"Here we go," said Reed. "The old and bold."

"In the army," repeated Green, "all the cookhouses have reserve stocks of bully beef, though they normally feed the troops on fresh meat. But every six months word goes out from on high to turn the bully over. That means that for about a week every meal is bully beef—tinned equivalent, they call it. Then the shelves are restocked with more tins of the same."

"Go on," said Masters.

"A year or two ago," said Green, "some chap discovered some tins of bully left over from the Boer War. They were literally eighty years old."

"And?"

"They were opened and sampled. The meat was in perfect condition—after eighty years."

"I get the point," said Masters.

"I'll be damned if I do," said Reed.

"You weren't meant to, lad," said Green. He took the rock cake from his plate, broke a piece off and held it down so that the dog could take it from his fingers. After it was gone, he said to the table at large. "This rock cake may be about eighty years old, too, but as the dog has eaten the sample, it should be safe for me to have the rest."

A moment or two later, Masters said: "Thanks, Bill. That's clarified it for me." He got to his feet. "Don't hurry. I'll meet you at the car."

Masters dropped a note on the table and walked out. Green got up to follow him. The others watched them go. As soon as they were out of the door, Betty Prior asked: "What was all that about?"

Reed said quietly: "It means it's all over."

"What is?"

"He's cracked it," said Berger.

"Cracked what?"

"The case. He knows it all from A to Z and back again."

Betty Prior stared. "You mean he knows who killed Norman Boyce? Just like that?"

"You've got it, love."

"But he's done nothing except talk to a few people. He's done no . . . no investigating."

"Which shows how mistaken you can be," said Reed. "When the Chief says it's been clarified, it's bloody-well solved—by him. And he doesn't make mistakes."

"But it's so disappointing."

"How do you mean, love?"

"The end of the only murder investigation I've been involved in. One run by Scotland Yard, and it ends in a whimper. 'Thanks, Bill, that's clarified it for me.' That's all. We don't even know who he thinks has done it."

"Thinks? Knows, love."

"All right, knows."

"Come on," said Berger. "we'd better be after them."

When Green joined him, Masters said: "I've been a bit slow, Bill."

"Seeing we haven't been here forty-eight hours yet, that's a load of rubbish, George, and you know it. But if you want to claim you're a twit, tell me why, or are you including me, too?"

"I am," said Masters bluntly. "We've all been as blind as bats."

"Rubbish."

"Literally rubbish. Bonfires, in fact."

"Have you gone off your chump?"

"Yesterday morning, Betty Prior and the sergeants dealt with a bonfire which had been lit too close to the highway."

"I can still remember that far back."

"What sort of rubbish was it?"

"Cartons, boxes, that sort of thing."

"Domestic?"

"No. Shop rubbish."

"Right. Young Berger tried to get in the gate, remember, but he couldn't because it had been wedged at the bottom."

"The chap let him in eventually."

"That's right. Do you remember what he said?"

Green didn't have to think. "Oh yes. He said he'd got the accumulated rubbish of thirty years there, and he'd had to wedge the gate to stop people coming in to pick it over."

"Anything else?"

"He'd had one at lunchtime the Tuesday before." Green stopped in his tracks. "Oh, lor! I suppose it was our old pal Joe Howlett. That bonfire was only about forty yards away from the back of the fish shop. After he'd left there he . . . a heap like that, all old tins and cartons, would draw an old tramp in to snoop round like honey draws bees. And to clinch it, it was lunchtime when Joe was about there."

"Quite right," said Masters. "And it's even money he had a few minutes in which to look over that heap before the owner discovered him. Plenty of time to pick up and pocket a carton as big as a box of cigarettes."

"Certainly. But what are you saying, George?"

"We walked along the High Street yesterday afternoon. Past the front of that empty shop."

"What about it?"

"Think, Bill, think. What did Sutcliffe say—according to the reports we got yesterday morning—when he described what he was going to do after he left the station at noon on Tuesday?"

"He was coming down here to see Morton to get some medicine for his missus."

"And why was he coming all this way to see a chemist?"

"Because the one near the nick had just closed down," said Green flatly. "And the empty shop on the High Street is the empty chemist's shop and the rubbish in the garden is the accumulation of years in that shop and among that rubbish was a carton of ten, out-of-date but still potent, ampoules each containing two hundred milligrams of gold salt which Joe Howlett nicked and then proceeded to add to Miss Foulger's wine because she had come the old acid with him in court and he wanted to pay her back."

"That's it," said Masters. "Simple, isn't it? That silly woman, whose heart is probably twice life-size under normal conditions, has to show her authority by uttering words which, though probably justified, are so ill-chosen and wounding that, in one morning, she can arouse one man to the pitch of wanting to harm her and another to want to rob her, all of which sets in motion a train of events that ends in murder. You know, Bill, there's a lot to be said for a few good honest cuss words directed at backsliders—as opposed to sarcasm and satire."

"I'm with you all the way," said Green. "Now, I suppose we have to visit the old boy at the closed-down shop."

"I even recall his name," mourned Masters. "James Stanmore, M.P.S., Chemist and Druggist. It was in gold letters on the fascia board. I noted it when we sauntered past yesterday afternoon."

As the sergeants and W.P.C. Prior came towards them, Green said: "I wonder just how much that fish-wife's treatment of Howlett played a part in driving him to seek revenge on all women? She must have stirred him up more than enough to make him return to get his own back on her so soon, so probably she was the final straw in determining him to play his tricks on Foulger."

"Corby played her part," agreed Masters.

Chapter 8

IT WAS FIVE o'clock in the afternoon when Masters reported to the Chief Constable of Colesworth. Also present besides Masters' own colleagues were D.C.S. Crewkerne, C.S. Warne, Inspector Snell and—at Masters' request—Sergeant Watson, Constable Sutcliffe, W.P.C. Prior and Professor Haywood.

"You have brought Joe Howlett in, I hear," said Crewkerne.

"With the Chief Constable's agreement."

"Masters is going to put us all in the know," said the C.C. "I have asked him to do that because this murder has affected some of us here very intimately and others of us have had the pleasure and honour of working with the Chief Superintendent over the past couple of days. Would you, therefore, please go ahead, Mr Masters."

The report took a little time because the senior officers present—with the exception of the C.C., who had been briefed earlier—were as yet unaware of the nature of the toxic agent that had killed Boyce, and so Masters had to describe this in detail. For the rest, however, he glossed over the thought processes and deductions which had caused him to question Haywood, which had leached the information from Morton and which had caused him to recall the bonfire and its significance.

When he came to the end, he added: "Mr Stanmore, the retiring chemist, has stated that he did throw out on to the rubbish heap a box of ten two hundred milligram ampoules of sodium auro-thiomalate. They had lain unnoticed for years at the back of a shelf in some dark corner of his dispensary. He sold all his stocks of those drugs which were still within their shelf life. But there were a

167

few—the gold among them—which, because of their age, were unacceptable to other pharmacists."

"Damn careless of him to throw them on a heap in his garden, though," said Warne.

"Not quite as irresponsible as it may seem," replied Masters. "All the liquids, powders and tablets he had to dispose of were flushed away down the loo. But ampoules cannot be disposed of in that way. As we know, he intended to destroy them by fire. Unfortunately he hadn't counted on his rubbish heap becoming an attraction for a professional picker-over of such dumps as Joe Howlett."

But Warne persisted: "What if kids had got in there, before Howlett? They could have been killed."

"True. But that is the wisdom of hindsight talking. A piece of broken window pane which any householder may deposit in his garden would constitute a danger to marauding children, as do all sorts of garden sprays and tools."

Warne obviously wasn't happy with this point of view, but he did not pursue his point.

Crewkerne said: "I suppose somebody is combing that rubbish heap at the moment?"

"Of course. A little of it was burned, but none of it beyond recognition. It is being combed at the moment because we must ensure that the ampoules are no longer there. I think you will agree—having heard how scarce ampoules of this particular strength are these days—that it would be an unbelievable coincidence if another ten were to turn up in Colesworth at this particular time. But we must be sure. I would add that the dump will be guarded until it is disposed of."

Crewkerne nodded. "I was wondering why some of my people had been taken off for unspecified duties."

"Sorry, Aubrey," said the C.C. "I couldn't get hold of you when Masters asked."

"I promised him all the help he needed," said Crewkerne. "And if that's all he's asking, we're getting off lightly. But I would like to ask Masters one big question, about something that he didn't really explain fully."

"What's that exactly?" asked Masters.

"You've done a grand job in double-quick time. But from an outsider's point of view, it seemed as if you went about it from the outside in instead of the other way about."

"Exactly what I told him," said Green. "But he isn't daft. He had to break in somewhere."

"Right," said Crewkerne. "So how did you break in so soon, young Masters?"

"There was nothing magical about it," replied Masters. "Always one of the first questions one must ask is whether anybody apparently held a grudge against the victim. According to your local newspaper, Watson had a grudge because of his daughter and Sutcliffe had one because of the leniency of the court. But there was one other. I didn't know who it was. But somebody had enough of a grudge against Boyce to discredit him to Mr Snell. Now Mr Snell knows Joe Howlett—has known him for many years—as an eccentric but honest, sober man who places himself voluntarily into the hands of the local police when it suits him to do so, and thereafter co-operates amicably in what comes after.

"But I suggest Mr Snell has only ever met Howlett when he, Howlett, is the suppliant succeeding in his aims. Never before has he met Howlett when the tramp's designs have been thwarted. So Mr Snell's picture of Howlett is incomplete; only half a portrait. And he judges the man on what he knows of him. That means he could not believe that Howlett would bear a grudge, even though he told tales to the police about Boyce and his friends. Mr Snell believed the information was given to him out of some sort of regard for the police, not out of pique engendered by a ticking-off from the bench, coupled with a refusal by the magistrates to sentence him. But I am a stranger here. I know nothing of Howlett. Consequently, when I heard that Howlett had grassed on Boyce, I treated it as though the squeal sprang from a genuine dislike of the lad. And that is where I broke into the circle. In the event, I was wrong. Howlett spoke out of anger and pique, like a small child in a tantrum lashing out at whatever is nearest, as opposed to speaking out of dislike of Boyce. But it didn't matter. It was the door that let me in to begin nosing round."

"And you did that before you knew what the Professor had to tell you?" asked Crewkerne.

"Yes. The toxic substance was important as were the amounts of it in the body and all the other forensic details. But really and truly, whatever the poison turned out to be merely affected the tracing of the substance, not the motives behind its use. That the two problems were intertwined merely meant that the unravelling of both could be done simultaneously."

"But, Chief," said Betty Prior, colouring as the heads of her own senior officers turned towards her. "Mr Green told you some story about a tin of bully beef that had been left over from the Boer War being still safe to eat. It had no relevance to any case, and yet you could make a decision about a murder in Colesworth because of his story."

"What exactly is your point, Betty?"

"Well, Chief, it just doesn't seem like criminal investigation to me. It's . . . well, it's more like a trick."

Masters smiled. "You are misjudging the part Mr Green played. He was on the same wavelength as myself throughout. At just the right time, when he could see I was struggling with some point, the solution to which seemed obvious to him, he gave me his advice by telling me a pertinent story. Had he made a bald statement of his beliefs, it might possibly have not been so convincing. He knew that, so he authenticated his advice by telling an anecdote about a situation that paralleled our own. You do much the same all the time—in essence—when you compare one crime with a similar one."

"That's right, lass," said Green. "We went to a cake shop for a chat, remember. We went because Sergeant Watson had told us Howlett went there last Tuesday. You were there with us. You heard how we were able to make use of the shop assistant's knowledge of Howlett's habits. The Chief Super told you, and the rest of us, that the info he got there suggested that old Joe had fouled Mrs Corby's wellies. But we understood, where you didn't, that if that were true, then it meant that Howlett was still in a revengeful mood on Tuesday night. So, if he was still in a mood to do the dirty on Mrs Corby so late at night, how much more likely was he to have done the dirty on Miss Foulger some hours earlier, before his anger had had any time at all to cool off? You can't explain this sort of team thinking and understanding because they only come with working together over a long time. And remember, too, that every team is different."

"Right," said Crewkerne. "And it depends on how lucky a team is in its separate members fitting in together. Any team can get a long way by working by the book and sticking to routine. But when everybody concerned is prepared to work in one particular way—whether by the book or, as in this case by leaning heavily on expertise and experience—then the team is liable to go further, quicker."

Snell spoke up.

"Have you charged Howlett with murder, Mr Masters?"

"Not yet. But he will have to be charged very soon. He has made a statement—a co-operative one as you would expect."

"But it won't be murder, will it?"

"Why not?"

"Because the intent was not there. He did not intend to kill Boyce."

"He intended to kill," said Masters. "Furthermore, it was a planned operation. He stole the means of encompassing death. He worked stealthily. He went to the house specifically to plant a toxic substance. He took care to remove the empty ampoules—even though he was careless enough to drop the snapped tops. All those factors show intent to kill by stealth. Who the victim was is immaterial. His defence will undoubtedly be that he did not intend to kill Boyce. But the lad died as a result of Howlett's criminal activities. We must, therefore, charge him with murder. The legal authorities may lessen the charge. That is their business, not ours."

"When will you charge him?" asked the C.C.

"This evening, sir, unless you have any objections. The inquest is tomorrow at eleven, I believe?"

"Yes."

"I think Howlett should appear before the magistrates before that, sir. Say at ten o'clock. It will be a brief appearance, because

171

I've no doubt his solicitor will want to reserve his defence. Then we can go to the inquest with a man already charged. That should achieve two objects. It will curtail the inquest because the arrest of Howlett will have forestalled the verdict, and it will nail the press. It was because of intemperate reporting that we were brought here. Now is the opportunity to show the public how ridiculous the innuendoes about the police were. To this end, I hope the coroner will let Professor Haywood speak to exonerate your men totally, so that nobody can murmur the old saw that there's no smoke without fire and that we've arrested a harmless old tramp as a cover-up."

"I find that eminently satisfactory," said the Chief Constable.

"At least," said Green, "old Joe will get the prison sentence he wanted."

Tom Watson said: "I told him to behave himself or he'd get more than he bargained for."

Masters looked at Warne. "Perhaps Mr Snell could put the formal charge."

"I'd rather not," said Snell. "I mean . . . well, you know I know him."

"I'll do it myself," said Warne. "Now?"

"If you please. It is six o'clock and we might as well wrap this up for the night."

As Warne rose, the C.C. said: "Before we break up, I'd like to say thank you to Mr Masters, Mr Green and Sergeants Reed and Berger. They've done a magnificent job and all of us here are relieved to have the matter resolved so quickly."

"Hear, hear," said Haywood. "I've found it fascinating—and educational."

Masters murmured something about it having been a pleasure. Green, already on his feet, said: "You'd have done it yourselves easily enough. The trouble was you were knocked sideways because the lad died in one of your cells. So you didn't spark quite soon enough."

"We thought the death was due to natural causes, Bill," said Crewkerne.

"I know, matey. And your police surgeon said the lad hadn't been knocked about, so you dismissed violence from your minds

—out of sheer relief, I suspect. And then that bloody reporter weighed in and effectively stopped you from taking any action. All I'm saying is that there should be some rule for us cops that says that every unexplained death is murder until it is proved not to be."

"I see your point," said Crewkerne heavily. "And I admit we should have been quicker off the mark. But . . ." He shrugged. "We're so taken up these days with keeping a good image that we don't do our job as we should. Leastways not always."

Masters smiled at Crewkerne. "That can't be right. At any rate as far as I know this is the first time the Yard has been called down to this neck of the woods, so the policing can't be all that bad." He looked around. "We shall see you all tomorrow morning. Mr Snell, you'll let me know what time the court is, and there's just one other thing."

"What's that, sir?"

"Make sure Miss Foulger isn't on the bench. Your magistrates will all have to be unconnected with the case."

"We'll make sure all three are different."

"Good."

When they were once more alone, Masters said to Reed, "You and Berger are free. You're taking Pam Watson out. Why not ask Betty Prior to make a foursome?"

"Good idea, Chief. Thanks. But is there any particular reason . . . ?"

"Just to say thank you to Betty and because whenever male police officers are dealing with women, it's as well to have a W.P.C. in attendance. It's more seemly and, I think, Tom Watson and his missus would think it was."

"I see. It's not a duty job then?"

"Oh, but it is. I want that girl treated so chivalrously that it will complete her re-education about coppers. By tomorrow I want her thinking that policemen are the goods and that her father—in her eyes—is once more a god among men."

"Got it, Chief. What will you be doing?"

"I think the D.C.I. and I have decided to ask Tom Watson and his missus round for a drink, haven't we, Bill?"

"We have that. Young Sutcliffe says his missus is feeling better now, so I've asked them, too. Just to restore morale, like."

Masters grinned. "None of your rhyming games tonight."

"No pitch, patch, pepper?"

"Skip it."

Masters wandered towards the door. As he reached it, he turned to face Green. "In the version of that flea one that I used to know, the last line was 'Here comes father with his shirt hanging out'. No mention of his tongue hanging out—as Haywood quoted it."

"Well, I'll be damned," said Green. "I wouldn't have thought you'd have known anything about it."

They walked out of the recreation room together. "Both versions could be apposite," said Masters. "It all depends how one views the situation."

"Right. He could have come along with his shirt hanging out because he'd dashed in to see what his missus was caterwauling about—interrupted in his toilette, you might say. Or he could have barged in with his tongue hanging out because he was thirsty and he was a bit put out at the prospect of not getting any tea—the flea having escaped."

Berger and Reed were following them. Reed turned to Berger, lifted his eyes in mock despair and whispered: "Senior detectives! I ask you! The tongue or shirt-tail mystery!"

"And this pitch, patch, pepper business. What's all that about?"

"I can't say exactly, but I do know that peppers—in that context—are very fast jumps when skipping."

"In that case, well, the Chief did a few peppers himself. Quick skips to a solution, you might say."

174

THE PERENNIAL LIBRARY MYSTERY SERIES

Delano Ames

CORPSE DIPLOMATIQUE   P 637, $2.84
"Sprightly and intelligent."
                    —*New York Herald Tribune Book Review*

FOR OLD CRIME'S SAKE   P 629, $2.84

MURDER, MAESTRO, PLEASE   P 630, $2.84
"If there is a more engaging couple in modern fiction than Jane and
Dagobert Brown, we have not met them."   —*Scotsman*

SHE SHALL HAVE MURDER   P 638, $2.84
"Combines the merit of both the English and American schools in the
new mystery. It's as breezy as the best of the American ones, and has
the sophistication and wit of any top-notch Britisher."
                    —*New York Herald Tribune Book Review*

E. C. Bentley

TRENT'S LAST CASE   P 440, $2.50
"One of the three best detective stories ever written."
                    —Agatha Christie

TRENT'S OWN CASE   P 516, $2.25
"I won't waste time saying that the plot is sound and the detection
satisfying. Trent has not altered a scrap and reappears with all his old
humor and charm."   —Dorothy L. Sayers

Gavin Black

A DRAGON FOR CHRISTMAS   P 473, $1.95
"Potent excitement!"   —*New York Herald Tribune*

THE EYES AROUND ME   P 485, $1.95
"I stayed up until all hours last night reading *The Eyes Around Me*,
which is something I do not do very often, but I was so intrigued by the
ingeniousness of Mr. Black's plotting and the witty way in which he spins
his mystery. I can only say that I enjoyed the book enormously."
                    —F. van Wyck Mason

YOU WANT TO DIE, JOHNNY?   P 472, $1.95
"Gavin Black doesn't just develop a pressure plot in suspense, he adds
uninfected wit, character, charm, and sharp knowledge of the Far East
to make rereading as keen as the first race-through."   —*Book Week*

THOU SHELL OF DEATH P 428, $1.95

"It has all the virtues of culture, intelligence and sensibility that the most exacting connoisseur could ask of detective fiction."

—*The Times* [London] *Literary Supplement*

THE WIDOW'S CRUISE P 399, $2.25

"A stirring suspense. . . . The thrilling tale leaves nothing to be desired."

—*Springfield Republican*

THE WORM OF DEATH P 400, $2.25

"It [The Worm of Death] is one of Blake's very best—and his best is better than almost anyone's." —Louis Untermeyer

John & Emery Bonett

A BANNER FOR PEGASUS P 554, $2.40

"A gem! Beautifully plotted and set. . . . Not only is the murder adroit and deserved, and the detection competent, but the love story is charming." —Jacques Barzun and Wendell Hertig Taylor

DEAD LION P 563, $2.40

"A clever plot, authentic background and interesting characters highly recommended this one." —*New Republic*

Christianna Brand

GREEN FOR DANGER P 551, $2.50

"You have to reach for the greatest of Great Names (Christie, Carr, Queen . . .) to find Brand's rivals in the devious subtleties of the trade."

—Anthony Boucher

TOUR DE FORCE P 572, $2.40

"Complete with traps for the over-ingenious, a double-reverse surprise ending and a key clue planted so fairly and obviously that you completely overlook it. If that's your idea of perfect entertainment, then seize at once upon *Tour de Force.*" —Anthony Boucher, *The New York Times*

James Byrom

OR BE HE DEAD P 585, $2.84

"A very original tale . . . Well written and steadily entertaining."

—Jacques Barzun & Wendell Hertig Taylor, *A Catalogue of Crime*

Henry Calvin

IT'S DIFFERENT ABROAD   P 640, $2.84
"What is remarkable and delightful, Mr. Calvin imparts a flavor of satire to what he renovates and compels us to take straight."
—Jacques Barzun

Marjorie Carleton

VANISHED   P 559, $2.40
"Exceptional . . . a minor triumph."
—Jacques Barzun and Wendell Hertig Taylor, *A Catalogue of Crime*

George Harmon Coxe

MURDER WITH PICTURES   P 527, $2.25
"[Coxe] has hit the bull's-eye with his first shot."
—*The New York Times*

Edmund Crispin

BURIED FOR PLEASURE   P 506, $2.50
"Absolute and unalloyed delight."
—Anthony Boucher, *The New York Times*

Lionel Davidson

THE MENORAH MEN   P 592, $2.84
"Of his fellow thriller writers, only John Le Carré shows the same instinct for the viscera."   —*Chicago Tribune*

NIGHT OF WENCESLAS   P 595, $2.84
"A most ingenious thriller, so enriched with style, wit, and a sense of serious comedy that it all but transcends its kind."
—*The New Yorker*

THE ROSE OF TIBET   P 593, $2.84
"I hadn't realized how much I missed the genuine Adventure story . . . until I read *The Rose of Tibet*."   —Graham Greene

D. M. Devine

MY BROTHER'S KILLER   P 558, $2.40
"A most enjoyable crime story which I enjoyed reading down to the last moment."   —Agatha Christie

Kenneth Fearing

THE BIG CLOCK   P 500, $1.95

"It will be some time before chill-hungry clients meet again so rare a compound of irony, satire, and icy-fingered narrative. *The Big Clock* is . . . a psychothriller you won't put down."   —*Weekly Book Review*

Andrew Garve

THE ASHES OF LODA   P 430, $1.50

"Garve . . . embellishes a fine fast adventure story with a more credible picture of the U.S.S.R. than is offered in most thrillers."

        —*The New York Times Book Review*

THE CUCKOO LINE AFFAIR   P 451, $1.95

". . . an agreeable and ingenious piece of work."   —*The New Yorker*

A HERO FOR LEANDA   P 429, $1.50

"One can trust Mr. Garve to put a fresh twist to any situation, and the ending is really a lovely surprise."   —*The Manchester Guardian*

MURDER THROUGH THE LOOKING GLASS   P 449, $1.95

". . . refreshingly out-of-the-way and enjoyable . . . highly recommended to all comers."   —*Saturday Review*

NO TEARS FOR HILDA   P 441, $1.95

"It starts fine and finishes finer. I got behind on breathing watching Max get not only his man but his woman, too."   —Rex Stout

THE RIDDLE OF SAMSON   P 450, $1.95

"The story is an excellent one, the people are quite likable, and the writing is superior."   —*Springfield Republican*

Michael Gilbert

BLOOD AND JUDGMENT   P 446, $1.95

"Gilbert readers need scarcely be told that the characters all come alive at first sight, and that his surpassing talent for narration enhances any plot. . . . Don't miss."   —*San Francisco Chronicle*

THE BODY OF A GIRL   P 459, $1.95

"Does what a good mystery should do: open up into all kinds of ramifications, with untold menace behind the action. At the end, there is a bang-up climax, and it is a pleasure to see how skilfully Gilbert wraps everything up."   —*The New York Times Book Review*

Michael Gilbert (cont'd)

THE DANGER WITHIN   P 448, $1.95
"Michael Gilbert has nicely combined some elements of the straight detective story with plenty of action, suspense, and adventure, to produce a superior thriller."   *—Saturday Review*

FEAR TO TREAD   P 458, $1.95
"Merits serious consideration as a work of art."
        —The New York Times

Joe Gores

HAMMETT   P 631, $2.84
"Joe Gores at his very best. Terse, powerful writing—with the master, Dashiell Hammett, as the protagonist in a novel I think he would have been proud to call his own."   —Robert Ludlum

C. W. Grafton

BEYOND A REASONABLE DOUBT   P 519, $1.95
"A very ingenious tale of murder . . . a brilliant and gripping narrative."
        —Jacques Barzun and Wendell Hertig Taylor

THE RAT BEGAN TO GNAW THE ROPE   P 639, $2.84
"Fast, humorous story with flashes of brilliance."
        —The New Yorker

Edward Grierson

THE SECOND MAN   P 528, $2.25
"One of the best trial-testimony books to have come along in quite a while."   *—The New Yorker*

Bruce Hamilton

TOO MUCH OF WATER   P 635, $2.84
"A superb sea mystery. . . . The prose is excellent."
        —Jacques Barzun and Wendell Hertig Taylor, *A Catalogue of Crime*

Cyril Hare

DEATH IS NO SPORTSMAN   P 555, $2.40
"You will be thrilled because it succeeds in placing an ingenious story in a new and refreshing setting. . . . The identity of the murderer is really a surprise."   *—Daily Mirror*

DEATH WALKS THE WOODS   P 556, $2.40
"Here is a fine formal detective story, with a technically brilliant solution demanding the attention of all connoisseurs of construction."
                    —Anthony Boucher, *The New York Times Book Review*

AN ENGLISH MURDER   P 455, $2.50
"By a long shot, the best crime story I have read for a long time. Everything is traditional, but originality does not suffer. The setting is perfect. Full marks to Mr. Hare."   —*Irish Press*

SUICIDE EXCEPTED   P 636, $2.84
"Adroit in its manipulation . . . and distinguished by a plot-twister which I'll wager Christie wishes she'd thought of."
                    —*The New York Times*

TENANT FOR DEATH   P 570, $2.84
"The way in which an air of probability is combined both with clear, terse narrative and with a good deal of subtle suburban atmosphere, proves the extreme skill of the writer."   —*The Spectator*

TRAGEDY AT LAW   P 522, $2.25
"An extremely urbane and well-written detective story."
                    —*The New York Times*

UNTIMELY DEATH   P 514, $2.25
"The English detective story at its quiet best, meticulously underplayed, rich in perceivings of the droll human animal and ready at the last with a neat surprise which has been there all the while had we but wits to see it."   —*New York Herald Tribune Book Review*

THE WIND BLOWS DEATH   P 589, $2.84
"A plot compounded of musical knowledge, a Dickens allusion, and a subtle point in law is related with delightfully unobtrusive wit, warmth, and style."   —*The New York Times*

WITH A BARE BODKIN   P 523, $2.25
"One of the best detective stories published for a long time."
                    —*The Spectator*

Robert Harling

THE ENORMOUS SHADOW   P 545, $2.50
"In some ways the best spy story of the modern period. . . . The writing is terse and vivid . . . the ending full of action . . . altogether first-rate."
—Jacques Barzun and Wendell Hertig Taylor, *A Catalogue of Crime*

Matthew Head

THE CABINDA AFFAIR P 541, $2.25
"An absorbing whodunit and a distinguished novel of atmosphere."
—Anthony Boucher, *The New York Times*

THE CONGO VENUS P 597, $2.84
"Terrific. The dialogue is just plain wonderful."
—*The Boston Globe*

MURDER AT THE FLEA CLUB P 542, $2.50
"The true delight is in Head's style, its limpid ease combined with humor and an awesome precision of phrase." —*San Francisco Chronicle*

M. V. Heberden

ENGAGED TO MURDER P 533, $2.25
"Smooth plotting." —*The New York Times*

James Hilton

WAS IT MURDER? P 501, $1.95
"The story is well planned and well written."
—*The New York Times*

P. M. Hubbard

HIGH TIDE P 571, $2.40
"A smooth elaboration of mounting horror and danger."
—*Library Journal*

Elspeth Huxley

THE AFRICAN POISON MURDERS P 540, $2.25
"Obscure venom, manical mutilations, deadly bush fire, thrilling climax compose major opus.... Top-flight."
—*Saturday Review of Literature*

MURDER ON SAFARI P 587, $2.84
"Right now we'd call Mrs. Huxley a dangerous rival to Agatha Christie." —*Books*

Francis Iles

BEFORE THE FACT P 517, $2.50

"Not many 'serious' novelists have produced character studies to compare with Iles's internally terrifying portrait of the murderer in *Before the Fact*, his masterpiece and a work truly deserving the appellation of unique and beyond price."
—Howard Haycraft

MALICE AFORETHOUGHT P 532, $1.95

"It is a long time since I have read anything so good as *Malice Aforethought*, with its cynical humour, acute criminology, plausible detail and rapid movement. It makes you hug yourself with pleasure."
—H. C. Harwood, *Saturday Review*

Michael Innes

THE CASE OF THE JOURNEYING BOY P 632, $3.12

"I could see no faults in it. There is no one to compare with him."
—*Illustrated London News*

DEATH BY WATER P 574, $2.40

"The amount of ironic social criticism and deft characterization of scenes and people would serve another author for six books."
—Jacques Barzun and Wendell Hertig Taylor

HARE SITTING UP P 590, $2.84

"There is hardly anyone (in mysteries or mainstream) more exquisitely literate, allusive and Jamesian—and hardly anyone with a firmer sense of melodramatic plot or a more vigorous gift of storytelling."
—Anthony Boucher, *The New York Times*

THE LONG FAREWELL P 575, $2.40

"A model of the deft, classic detective story, told in the most wittily diverting prose."
—*The New York Times*

THE MAN FROM THE SEA P 591, $2.84

"The pace is brisk, the adventures exciting and excitingly told, and above all he keeps to the very end the interesting ambiguity of the man from the sea."
—*New Statesman*

THE SECRET VANGUARD P 584, $2.84

"Innes . . . has mastered the art of swift, exciting and well-organized narrative."
—*The New York Times*

THE WEIGHT OF THE EVIDENCE P 633, $2.84

"First-class puzzle, deftly solved. University background interesting and amusing."
—*Saturday Review of Literature*

Mary Kelly

THE SPOILT KILL P 565, $2.40
"Mary Kelly is a new Dorothy Sayers. . . . [An] exciting new novel."
—*Evening News*

Lange Lewis

THE BIRTHDAY MURDER P 518, $1.95
"Almost perfect in its playlike purity and delightful prose."
—Jacques Barzun and Wendell Hertig Taylor

Allan MacKinnon

HOUSE OF DARKNESS P 582, $2.84
"His best . . . a perfect compendium."
—Jacques Barzun & Wendell Hertig Taylor, *A Catalogue of Crime*

Arthur Maling

LUCKY DEVIL P 482, $1.95
"The plot unravels at a fast clip, the writing is breezy and Maling's approach is as fresh as today's stockmarket quotes."
—*Louisville Courier Journal*

RIPOFF P 483, $1.95
"A swiftly paced story of today's big business is larded with intrigue as a Ralph Nader-type investigates an insurance scandal and is soon on the run from a hired gun and his brother. . . . Engrossing and credible."
—*Booklist*

SCHROEDER'S GAME P 484, $1.95
"As the title indicates, this Schroeder is up to something, and the unravelling of his game is a diverting and sufficiently blood-soaked entertainment."
—*The New Yorker*

Austin Ripley

MINUTE MYSTERIES P 387, $2.50
More than one hundred of the world's shortest detective stories. Only one possible solution to each case!

Thomas Sterling

THE EVIL OF THE DAY P 529, $2.50
"Prose as witty and subtle as it is sharp and clear. . .characters unconventionally conceived and richly bodied forth . . . . In short, a novel to be treasured."
—Anthony Boucher, *The New York Times*

Julian Symons

THE BELTING INHERITANCE P 468, $1.95

"A superb whodunit in the best tradition of the detective story."
—August Derleth, *Madison Capital Times*

BLAND BEGINNING P 469, $1.95

"Mr. Symons displays a deft storytelling skill, a quiet and literate wit, nice feeling for character, and detectival ingenuity of a high order."
—Anthony Boucher, *The New York Times*

ROGUE'S FORTUNE P 481, $1.95

"There's a touch of the old sardonic humour, and more than a touch of style." —*The Spectator*

THE BROKEN PENNY P 480, $1.95

"The most exciting, astonishing and believable spy story to appear in years. —Anthony Boucher, *The New York Times Book Review*

THE COLOR OF MURDER P 461, $1.95

"A singularly unostentatious and memorably brilliant detective story."
—*New York Herald Tribune Book Review*

Dorothy Stockbridge Tillet
(John Stephen Strange)

THE MAN WHO KILLED FORTESCUE P 536, $2.25

"Better than average." —*Saturday Review of Literature*

Simon Troy

THE ROAD TO RHUINE P 583, $2.84

"Unusual and agreeably told." —*San Francisco Chronicle*

SWIFT TO ITS CLOSE P 546, $2.40

"A nicely literate British mystery . . . the atmosphere and the plot are exceptionally well wrought, the dialogue excellent." —*Best Sellers*

Henry Wade

THE DUKE OF YORK'S STEPS P 588, $2.84

"A classic of the golden age."
—Jacques Barzun & Wendell Hertig Taylor, *A Catalogue of Crime*

A DYING FALL P 543, $2.50

"One of those expert British suspense jobs . . . it crackles with undercurrents of blackmail, violent passion and murder. Topnotch in its class."
—*Time*

Henry Wade (cont'd)

THE HANGING CAPTAIN   P 548, $2.50

"This is a detective story for connoisseurs, for those who value clear thinking and good writing above mere ingenuity and easy thrills."

—*Times Literary Supplement*

Hillary Waugh

LAST SEEN WEARING . . .   P 552, $2.40

"A brilliant tour de force."   —Julian Symons

THE MISSING MAN   P 553, $2.40

"The quiet detailed police work of Chief Fred C. Fellows, Stockford, Conn., is at its best in *The Missing Man* . . . one of the Chief's toughest cases and one of the best handled."

—Anthony Boucher, *The New York Times Book Review*

Henry Kitchell Webster

WHO IS THE NEXT?   P 539, $2.25

"A double murder, private-plane piloting, a neat impersonation, and a delicate courtship are adroitly combined by a writer who knows how to use the language."   —Jacques Barzun and Wendell Hertig Taylor

Anna Mary Wells

MURDERER'S CHOICE   P 534, $2.50

"Good writing, ample action, and excellent character work."

—*Saturday Review of Literature*

A TALENT FOR MURDER   P 535, $2.25

"The discovery of the villain is a decided shock."   —*Books*

Edward Young

THE FIFTH PASSENGER   P 544, $2.25

"Clever and adroit . . . excellent thriller . . ."   —*Library Journal*

If you enjoyed this book you'll want to know about
THE PERENNIAL LIBRARY MYSTERY SERIES

Buy them at your local bookstore or use this coupon for ordering:

Qty	P number	Price

postage and handling charge		$1.00
_____ book(s) @ $0.25		_____
	TOTAL	

Prices contained in this coupon are Harper & Row invoice prices only.
They are subject to change without notice, and in no way reflect the prices at
which these books may be sold by other suppliers.

**HARPER & ROW, Mail Order Dept. #PMS, 10 East 53rd St., New
York, N.Y. 10022.**
Please send me the books I have checked above. I am enclosing $_____
which includes a postage and handling charge of $1.00 for the first book and
25¢ for each additional book. Send check or money order. No cash or
C.O.D.s please

Name_____

Address_____

City_____ State_____ Zip_____

Please allow 4 weeks for delivery. USA only. This offer expires 10/31/84.
Please add applicable sales tax.